SATAN
YOU <u>CAN'T</u>
HAVE
ISRAEL

#1 *NEW YORK TIMES* BESTSELLING AUTHOR

MIKE EVANS

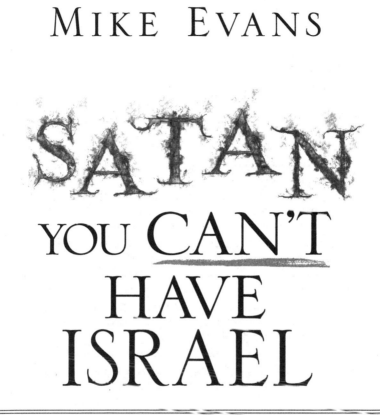

SATAN
YOU CAN'T
HAVE
ISRAEL

A SPIRITUAL WARFARE GUIDE TO SAVE ISRAEL

TIMEWORTHY
·BOOKS·

P.O. BOX 30000, PHOENIX, AZ 85046

This book is dedicated to my beloved mother,
Jean Jennie Levine,
who taught me to love the Jewish people.

She revealed the history of anti-Semitism family members
had experienced—especially that of her grandfather,
Rabbi Mikael Katz-Nelson from Minsk, Belarus.
He and his entire congregation were burned to death
in their wooden synagogue. The crowd outside boarded
the doors and lit a fire while screaming, "Christ killers."

As a child, I saw anti-Semitism first-hand:
eggs and tomatoes were thrown at my mother
while she was taunted with the words "Jew witch."
Even worse, between 1:00 and 2:00 AM on
Saturday mornings, my anti-Semitic father would
sit her in a chair at the bottom of the stairs, slam her in
the face, and scream over and over, "You Jew whore!
That #*&@# upstairs is not my son! He's a $*&^% of the
affair you had with that Jew while I was in the army."

It was my mother who nurtured my love for the
Jewish people.

PREFACE 9

1 ISRAEL IS GOD'S DREAM 19

2 THE BLESSINGS AND CURSES OF GOD 29

3 JERUSALEM, THE HEART AND SOUL
OF THE EARTH 43

4 JERUSALEM'S SPIRITUAL SIGNIFICANCE 57

5 GOD'S WORD IS IMMUTABLE 69

6 SALVATION IS OF THE JEWS 81

7 GOD ABHORS ANTI-SEMITISM 91

8 COMFORT ISRAEL 99

9 SILENCE IMPLIES CONSENT 115

10 GOD ALMIGHTY HAS PRESERVED ISRAEL 129

11 BLESSINGS ABUNDANTLY 141

12 THE VALUE OF INTERCESSORS 165

AFTERWORD: STAND WITH ISRAEL 175

ENDNOTES 193

APPENDIX: MAPS 193

AUTHOR BIO 201

PSALM 102:12-22

But You, O Lord, shall endure forever,
And the remembrance of Your name to all generations.
You will arise *and* have mercy on Zion;
For the time to favor her,
Yes, the set time, has come.
For Your servants take pleasure in her stones,
And show favor to her dust.
So the nations shall fear the name of the Lord,
And all the kings of the earth Your glory.
For the Lord shall build up Zion;
He shall appear in His glory.
He shall regard the prayer of the destitute,
And shall not despise their prayer. (NKJV)

PREFACE

ISRAEL IS UNDER ATTACK. It is ground zero in the eyes of Middle East radical Islam. At the same time, the oil-appeasing nations of the world are putting indescribable pressure on tiny Israel to make concessions to a terror regime—the PLO that represents the Palestinians and is punishing Israel globally through economic boycotts and demonization. Israel is being pressured to give up the vast majority of Judea and Samaria, its Bible lands, as well as East Jerusalem in order to appease Islamic rage.

The peace plan that has been put forth calls for East Jerusalem, part of the capital city of the State of Israel and the home of Christianity, to become the Islamic capital of a Palestinian state. The payment for this is the promise that the Palestinian Authority will acknowledge Israel's right of survival as a Jewish state.

In early 2015, I spent an hour with former President George W. Bush and former Israeli President Shimon Peres at the Bush Presidential Library in Dallas, Texas.

Mr. Peres was to present the former president with an award from The Friends of Zion Heritage Center and Museum, which I founded.

President Peres, the ninth president of Israel, is the most beloved Jewish leader worldwide. He served twice as prime minister, is a Nobel Peace Prize winner, and has done everything he possibly could during his lifetime to show tolerance and respect. Despite that, the adversaries of Israel have continued with their terror attacks and global incitement.

The battle for Jerusalem has gone on for more than 6,000 years—since the day Abraham pitched his tent on Mount Zion and made a covenant with God. Islamic dictators control over 13 million square kilometers in the Middle East. The Islamic world wants to add Palestine as its twenty-second state, with East Jerusalem as its capital.

Prime Minister Menachem Begin, to whom I served as a confidant told me that when he went to Camp David in 1978 to make peace with Egypt, President Carter warned him that the United States did not recognize Jerusalem as Israel's capital. Begin answered, "Whether you recognize Jerusalem or don't recognize Jerusalem, it is the capital of the State of Israel."

In Zechariah 12, the prophet declared, "I will seek to destroy all the nations that come against Jerusalem." This prediction has held true throughout history for all nations that have come against the Jewish people: Empires such as the British and the Roman are no more. The greatest curse of all will come, as it always has in the past, upon the nation that comes against Jerusalem.

The Holy City is the home of the Temple site—which has become ground zero for spiritual warfare. Like the Great Whore of Babylon, principalities and powers roar across the earth attempting to seduce the nations. Jerusalem remains the apple of God's eye, His diadem, His firstborn, His chosen, His beloved, the jewel in His crown.

In Joel 3:16, NIV, God declares: "The Lord will roar from Zion and thunder from Jerusalem; the earth and the heavens will tremble. But the Lord will be a refuge for His people, a stronghold for the people of Israel."

In 1980 I wrote a book entitled *Israel, America's Key to Survival.* On the cover of the book was a picture of the American flag being slashed by a Saudi Scimitar. I believed then, and still do, that if the state of Israel is weakened, radical Islam will invade the West and attack the United States, and that the first terrorist attack will come at the hands of Saudis. (Fifteen of the nineteen hijackers involved in the September 11, 2001 attacks were Saudi citizens.)

The truth is, anti-Semitism is alive and well on Planet Earth. Nothing has assuaged that which erupted the moment God declared a covenant with Abraham and his offspring. The UN and a large percentage of the world consider Israel to be a racist, occupying state. Rallying behind the Palestinians is today a politically correct way of hating Israel and assisting those who seek her obliteration. Israel is a lightning rod for worldwide anti-Semitism. Rather than attack a Jew, anti-Semites now attack the collective Jew, Israel, while hiding behind the cloak of what passes as social justice.

Rather than attack militarily and start an unwinnable war, Israel's Arab neighbors have fashioned a new strategy: Asymmetrical terrorism. It is defined as "a conflict in which a much weaker opponent uses unorthodox or surprise tactics to attack the weak points of the much stronger opponent, especially involving terrorism, guerilla warfare, and other strategies."[1] It worked for the Viet Cong in Vietnam with a strategy that forced the United States to slink away in ignominious defeat.

Even with such scurrilous attacks against Israel as the Arab-Israeli War following Israel's Declaration of Independence in 1948, The Six-Day War in 1967, the Yom Kippur War of 1973, the conflicts with Lebanon, Yasser Arafat's Intifadas from 1987 to 1993 and from 2000 to 2005, and the ongoing attacks from Hamas in Gaza, Israel has stood strong against her enemies. Therefore, the terrorists that surround the Land of the Bible have resorted to tactics of unrest and fear—knife attacks by Palestinian women and children; vehicular assaults, and other forms of terrorism. As if that weren't enough, Israel has in recent years been faced with increasing economic assaults from sources worldwide, and from ideological warfare.

For example, the media often try to make us believe that terrorism in Israel is the fault solely of the Israeli refusal to give away more land for peace. The Palestinians are painted as victims, thus only victims are morally entitled to whatever they can wrestle away from others. Consequently, only those infidels who align themselves with the victims are worthy of consideration. It is, therefore, better and more advantageous to be a victim. Terror demands, not a forceful response, but an apology for past unforgiven sins against the "victim." Too many times we have seen U.S.

leaders apologize to those who have wronged both Israel and Western countries.

My lifework has been to defend the Jewish people and the nation of Israel. For me, this is extremely personal. Why?

My late mother, Jean Levine, came from an Orthodox Jewish background. My understanding of Judaism was gleaned from her. She filled our home with all things Jewish: menorahs, Gefilte fish and other Jewish foods, and celebrations. I would hear her talking on the phone in Yiddish with her relatives.

My father was not Jewish; he was a professing Christian who faithfully attended church each Sunday where he was greeted as "Brother Bob." He just as faithfully visited the Twilight Café every Friday night to drink away the hours with his friends. He always walked because he knew he would not be able to drive home. When Dad finally returned between 1:00 and 2:00 AM, he would set my mother in a chair near the bottom of the stairs. In a drunken rage he would then batter her and scream that she was a Jewish whore while accusing her of having an affair with a Jewish man. He thought I was the product of the affair.

Many Sundays while he was at church praising the Lord, Mother would don sunglasses to hide her black eyes. My greatest shame was that I could not defend her against an anti-Semite. I attempted to do so one night as my father was again abusing my mother, and screamed, "Stop it!" He flew up the stairs, lifted me above his head by my throat and strangled me. He left me for dead on the floor.

This is why I am so determined to support the Jewish people. My love for my mother morphed into a love for her people. . . my people.

Satan has a definitive objective: to kill, steal and destroy. The devil's desire is to kill Jewish people, steal their birthright and destroy their land. Why? If he can destroy the offspring of Abraham, Isaac, and Jacob, Satan can negate the covenant on which the entire Bible was founded. This is why it is crucial that the Church of Jesus Christ raise the banner of prayer and intercession over the House of Israel.

Author and theologian The Reverend Simon Ponsonby of Saint Aldate's Church in Oxford noted:

> The Apostles would not recognise much in the church today. A Christianity divorced from its Jewish roots has always opened itself up to the demonic spirit of anti-Semitism.[2]

Not once did Jesus deny His Jewish heritage. The Bible

tells us that Mary and Joseph observed the ordinances for the birth of a baby—Jesus was circumcised on the eighth day; He observed the feasts of the Jews; He wore the tallit, the prayer shawl, when He prayed. He honored His brethren, and you and I are to do the same. For centuries Jewish people have seen only the harshness of those who profess to be Christians, yet too often practice anti-Semitism.

The time has come for you and me to practice loving acts of humanity toward the descendants of Abraham, Isaac, and Jacob.

> Then the King will say to those on his right, 'Come, you who are blessed by my Father; take your inheritance, the kingdom prepared for you since the creation of the world. For I was hungry and you gave me something to eat, I was thirsty and you gave me something to drink, I was a stranger and you invited me in, I needed clothes and you clothed me, I was sick and you looked after me, I was in prison and you came to visit me.' (Matthew 25:34-36, NIV)

PRAYER FOR ISRAEL:

Heavenly Father, Jehovah God,

The enemies of God continue to pursue Your Chosen People. Satan's desire is to annihilate the Jewish people. You have called Believers who have been grafted into the olive tree and who share in God's rich blessings to not sit idly on the sidelines, but to stand in unity with the Seed of Israel, the Root of Jesse. In these dark and decisive times, help me to "blow the trumpet in Zion and sound the alarm on God's holy mountain!" Let the redeemed of the Lord say so! Today, I choose to serve the Lord and intercede for the people of Israel. I stand and boldly declare, "Satan, you can't have Israel!"

SCRIPTURES FOR STUDY:

Joel 2:1	Psalm 107:2
Joshua 24:15	Genesis 12:1-3
Psalm 122:6	Zechariah 2:9
Joel 3:1-3	Psalm 144:1
Judges 2:1	Psalm 25:22

1

ISRAEL IS GOD'S DREAM

"The Lord said to Abram after Lot had parted from him, "Look around from where you are, to the north and south, to the east and west. All the land that you see I will give to you and your offspring forever. I will make your offspring like the dust of the earth, so that if anyone could count the dust, then your offspring could be counted. Go, walk through the length and breadth of the land, for I am giving it to you."

GENESIS 13:14-17, NIV

ISRAEL IS A TINY COUNTRY with a population of less than 8 million and a land mass comparable to the state of New Jersey—the fifth smallest state in the U.S. It is 290 miles in length and only 85 miles wide. Israel's role on the world stage should seemingly be relatively minor, yet hardly a day goes by when events in or concerning Israel do not dominate international headlines. What many today seem to overlook is that Israel didn't just rise from the rocky land of Palestine in 1948; it has been in existence for centuries although known by various names.

Columnist Charles Krauthammer wrote graphically of the land today:

> Israel is the very embodiment of Jewish continuity: It is the only nation on earth that inhabits the same land, bears the same name, speaks the same language, and worships the same God that it did 3,000 years ago. You dig the soil and you find pottery from Davidic times, coins from Bar Kokhba, and 2,000-year-old scrolls written in a script remarkably like the one that today advertises ice cream at the corner candy store.[3]

At the end of World War II with all its horrors of the Holocaust, the devastated Jewish survivors in Europe longed to travel to Palestine, their biblical homeland. Their dreams were to be delayed when Britain was placed in control of Palestine by mandate of the United Nations, and with a growing dilemma: How to walk the tightrope between world opinion and the Arabs. After the shock and revulsion of the Holocaust, much of the world increasingly demanded that the Jews be allowed to emigrate to Palestine—thought to be a place of safety for them. Arabs in the region were adamantly opposed to the move. Greatly frustrated by the situation, the British announced in February 1947 that control of Palestine would be ceded to the United Nations, even then a hotbed of anti-Semitism.

Journalist Eric R. Mandel wrote of the cultural relativism that still today grips the UN:

> Non-democratic states overwhelmingly control the UN. They often mouth the words of moderation, but defend nations that give sanctuary to terrorists. How else can one explain that some of the most odious nations on earth are elected to the UN Human Rights Council? In fact, Israel's judge and jury at the UN are often nations that enable terrorism and anti-Semitism.
>
> To accurately judge the United Nations, we need a definition. If Israel is treated and judged completely differently than other nations and held to a standard not applied to any other member nation, then that should be considered anti-Semitism.[4]

In November 1947, the UN offered a plan for partition that would divide the region into an Arab state and a

Jewish state, calling for British troops to leave Palestine by August 1948. The Jews welcomed the proposal; the Arabs scorned it. Some British leaders felt it would be impossible for a Jewish state to flourish in the face of such hostility from the Arabs.

In the interim, Jewish leaders moved forward with plans for statehood. A provisional government was established under David Ben-Gurion in March 1948. Two months later, on May 14, as Egyptian fighter-bombers roared overhead and British troops readied for departure, Ben-Gurion and his political partners gathered at the museum in Tel Aviv:

> At 16:00 [4:00 PM], Ben-Gurion opened the ceremony by banging his gavel on the table, prompting a spontaneous rendition of Hatikvah, soon to be Israel's national anthem, from the 250 guests.[5]

The following day, Israel was attacked by the Arab nations that ring her borders. Only through the grace and protection of God was Israel able to survive. Again and again over the years this tiny island of freedom has suffered assaults directed by evil men dedicated to the annihilation of the Jewish people.

Today Israel is more isolated than ever. Security is a never-ending struggle as all of Israel's neighbors either actively oppose her or at least harbor those who do. Terrorist groups thrive in Gaza, which shares Israel's border with Egypt and harbors Hamas. Lebanon is home to Hezbollah, which along with Hamas is an Iranian proxy. The ongoing Syrian civil war has opened the door to an influx of Iran's Revolutionary Guard, an avowed enemy of Israel, and to the Islamic State—the burgeoning enemy of all mankind. Since the reuniting of the city of Jerusalem, there have been over 10,000 terrorist attacks in the Bible land. There have been more suicide bombings in Jerusalem than in any other city in the world.

The direct result of demon-possessed rhetoric from mosques, madrassas and mullahs, has produced a plague of Palestinian men, women and children stabbing Israelis in the streets. These stabbings were incited in part by radical Islamic cleric Sheik Khaled Al-Mughrabi who broadcast lies that Israel planned to take control of the temple mount. Such bombastic outcries only serve to stir up more animosity for both Israel and the United States. Is it any wonder that ISIS has called for a plague of suicide bombers in its "Project Behead the Jews?"

As my dear friend Prime Minister Benjamin Netanyahu has repeatedly pointed out, the contention is not about a Palestinian state, or the division of Jerusalem, settlements, checkpoints, security fences, or borders. The issue is Israel's very right to exist as a nation. Most of the Arab world still refuses to accept this simple proposition.

Not only do these thugocracies think Israel has no right to exist as a *state*, they think the Jewish *people* have no right to survive. Their opposition to Israel's national aspirations has always been tied to the Muslim world's ultimate resistance to the right of the Jewish people to exist at all. Peaceful co-existence has never been the goal of the Arabs. Even having Jews living in other lands is not an option for fanatical Islamists and modern-day Neo-Nazis. Their real goal has been the abnegation, and in its worst and most absolute form, the very extermination, of the entire Jewish race.

This is why Palestinian children are taught to hate and kill Jews from their first breath and why the Islamic world throws parties in the streets every time Jewish blood is shed. This is why in radical Islamic theology the successful homicidal maiming and murder of Jews represents the highest aspirations many Palestinian mothers have for their children. The demons of hell dance every time a Jew is murdered.

Anti-Israeli sentiment has in fact become the new anti-Semitism. It makes Israel the new "collective Jew" which justifies assaults on individual Jews as the extension of the state. This hatred—not any other issue—is the true source of murder and terrorism.

Author George Gilder wrote of today's version of the Hitler youth movement:

> Today Hitler's rants have morphed into a global program of religious education and military ideology sustained by Arab and Iranian oil money. The hundreds of thousands of Brown Shirts in Germany have become millions of frothing jihadi youths similarly inculcated with anti-Semitic hatred and a lust for violence. Leading politicians in Iran, Egypt, Syria, Malaysia, Venezuela, and other nations, and jihadi imams and mullahs around the globe have declared their resolve to destroy Israel....Anti-Semites have the moral support of much of the UN bureaucracy, including its "human rights" apparatus, which is chiefly devoted to anti-Semitic [agitation propaganda.]... The UN Secretary General has called for a global boycott of Israel for its efforts to defend itself against

new campaigns of extermination. . . . Scores of nations, representing 1.8 billion Muslims, have endorsed jihad.[6]

The terror wars that Israel fights in the twenty-first century are not against a particular Arab nation. Rather, the conflict is spearheaded by an unpredictable and often unidentifiable band of terrorists with the ability and mobility to shift from country to country almost at will. Without identifying uniforms, they become invisible, striking without warning. The attacks are meant to instill fear and trepidation among the Jewish populace. This is one of the many reasons the U.S. alliance with Israel continues to be a necessity. We learned a harsh lesson on September 11, 2001: If terrorism is not contained in the Middle East, we can anticipate more attacks on the West.

Author David Naggar wrote:

> As for Israel, one either sees or does not see that Israel is on the front line of a war that pits the advancement of humankind against barbarism. One either sees or does not see that the fight in Afghanistan is the same as the fight in Iraq, and the same as the fight in Yemen and Somalia. The

Jihadists are using the whole global boxing ring. They are not confining the fight to the battle-grounds we dictate. Like the game whack-a-mole, if the seekers of liberty and human advancement seem to be gaining the upper hand in one part of the world, Jihadists will simply fold their tents at night and surface in another part of the world in the morning.[7]

The spiritual door was opened for the 9/11 attack against the U.S., primarily *because* the policy of the government has been to make demands and pressure the Israelis not to retaliate in a significant way against terrorist strikes launched against them. We must reverse that policy and stand with our closest ally in the Middle East—Israel!

In recent years, nations such as the United States of America, Canada, and Great Britain that long stood with Israel have moved away from their traditional support. They do so at their own peril because we are standing at a prophetic crossroads—one that will determine the future of our world. We must not fail to do our part to fight and win the battle for Israel's survival. We must stand toe-to-toe with the Enemy and shout: "Satan, You Can't Have God's People, Israel!"

PRAYER FOR ISRAEL:

Let them all be confounded and turned back that hate Zion. Let them be as grass upon the housetops, which withers before it grows up. Lord, deal justly and swiftly with Your enemies. Destroy and divide the tongues of those who would incite violence against Israel. In the name of Jesus, we bind every false religion and false doctrine that does not acknowledge Your eternal plan for the land and people of Israel. The scepter of the wicked will not remain over the land allotted to the righteous. Father, break the strongholds of religion, pride and wickedness that seek to control Israel. The Lord will not forsake His people for His great name's sake, because it has pleased the Lord to make Israel His people. The Lord brings the counsel of the nations to nothing; He makes their plans of no effect. We declare that God's purposes for Israel will be completely fulfilled and that He will be glorified. Show Your lovingkindness to Your people Israel and keep them as the apple of Your eye. Hide them under the shadow of Your wings, from the wicked who oppress them, from their deadly enemies who surround them.[8] In the Name of Jesus I declare: Satan, You Cannot Have Israel!"

SCRIPTURES FOR STUDY:

Psalm 129:5-6	Psalm 17:7-9	Psalm 33:10
1 Samuel 12:22	Psalm 125:3	Psalm 55:9
Jeremiah 31:10	II Samuel 7:24	Psalm 25:22
Jeremiah 33:9		

2

THE BLESSINGS AND CURSES OF GOD

"The LORD shall bless thee out of Zion: and thou shalt see the good of Jerusalem all the days of thy life."

PSALM 128:5, KJV

IN ZECHARIAH 2:8, God warns of the danger of offending Israel:

> For thus says the LORD of hosts: "He sent Me after glory, to the nations which plunder you; for he who touches you touches the apple of His eye."

Earlier in Genesis 12:1-3, God had assured Abraham that those who blessed Israel would be blessed, and that anyone who cursed Israel would be cursed. These three verses alone should be sufficient warning as to why we are called to support Israel:

The LORD had said to Abram, "Go from your country, your people and your father's household to the land I will show you. I will make you into a great nation, and I will bless you; I will make your name great, and you will be a blessing. I will bless those who bless you, and whoever curses you I will curse; and all peoples on earth will be blessed through you" (NIV.)

Hebrew writer Israel Matzav wrote about blessing and cursing:

One need not be a Jew or Christian or even believe in God to appreciate that this verse is as accurate a prediction as humanity has ever been given by the ancient world. The Jewish people have suffered longer and more horribly than any other living people. But they are still around. Its historic enemies are all gone. Those that cursed the Jews were indeed cursed. . . .Those who curse the Jews still seem to be cursed. The most benighted civilization today is the Arab world. One could make a plausible case that the Arab world's preoccupation with Jew-hatred and destroying Israel is a decisive factor in its failure to progress. The day the Arab world makes peace with the existence of the tiny Jewish state in its midst, the Arab world will begin its ascent. The converse is what worries tens of millions of Americans—the day America abandons Israel; America will begin its descent.[9]

In October 1991 during the Madrid Peace Conference, I stood gazing at the ceiling in the grand Hall of Columns in the Royal Palace in Madrid. It was ornately embellished with the images of pagan gods: Apollo, Aurora, Zephyrus, Ceres, Bacchus, Diana, Pan and Galatea. The beautiful interior was all glitter and no substance, a disguise for its actual purpose: the place where even more land-for-peace would be demanded of the Jews.

I can still hear their voices reverberating through the marble halls: "We will accept your land in exchange for peace." What they were really saying was: "This is a stick-up. Give me all your land and you won't get hurt—much." Muggings usually happen on the streets of major cities, but the Madrid Peace Conference, by any measure, was an international mugging. And the world was peopled by a silent majority too intimidated to report the crime to the police. Most of the nations represented pretended not to see the gun pointed at Israel's head.

At the end of the Peace Conference, Syria was awarded billions of dollars by the U.S. That was subsequently spent on the purchase of North Korean missiles to be used against Israel. Many of those missiles soon filtered into the hands of Hezbollah terrorists in Lebanon and have since been launched into Israeli towns and villages in various attacks on its northern cities. Conversely, Israel was penalized with the freeze of a $10 billion dollar loan guarantee, money needed to provide housing for Russian Jewish refugees.

The nations that ransacked, burned, leveled, and tried to obliterate the Jewish people are today rife with devastation. We have only to examine history to ascertain that the remnants of those once-great empires are now dust and ashes. Time after time since the beginning of her existence, nations have come against Israel. Yet, like the Phoenix, she has risen from the ashes each time. Not one ruler who ordered the destruction of Jerusalem long survived. Nebuchadnezzar conquered Jerusalem in 586 BC and then was doomed to live as a beast of the field for seven terrifying years. He was restored to sanity only after he recognized the God of the Israelites. (See Daniel 9) His kingdom of Babylon was conquered by Cyrus the Great.

In 332 BC Alexander the Great captured Jerusalem. His empire fragmented after his death, and the followers of Ptolemy in Egypt and then the Seleucids of Syria ruled over Jerusalem. The Jews, horrified by the desecration of the Temple under the Seleucid ruler, Antiochus IV, staged a revolt and regained independence under the Hasmonean Dynasty. That independence lasted one hundred years, until Pompey established Roman rule in the city. The Holy Roman Empire collapsed after the Temple was destroyed and Jerusalem was leveled.

The British, who ruled over Palestine and Jerusalem following World War I, could once boast that the sun never set on the British Empire. Indeed, one-fifth of the world's population was then under its rule. However, after turning away Jews from both Britain and Palestine when they fled Hitler's gas chambers, and after arming Arabs to fight against them in Palestine, the empire quickly began to disintegrate. Great Britain today is comprised of just fourteen territories, consisting of a number of islands. Gone are the days when that empire stretched from India to Canada and from Australia to Africa.

In 1939, Winston Churchill stood before Parliament in London and countered efforts to renounce support for a Jewish homeland. In his speech, he praised the work of those already in Palestine and then damned those who had come against the Jews already in the land:

> They [the Jews] have made the desert bloom. . . started a score of thriving industries. . . founded a great city on the barren shore. . . harnessed the Jordan and spread its electricity throughout the land. . . So far from being persecuted, the Arabs have crowded into the country and multiplied till their population has increased more. . . We are now asked to submit—and this is what rankles most with me—to an agitation which is fed with foreign money and ceaselessly inflamed by Nazi and Fascist propaganda.[10]

Little has changed; there are still many whose only agenda is to force the Jews from Israel—or annihilate them, if at all possible. Yet, Jerusalem and Israel remain standing as an unquestioned testimony to the determination and courage of the Jewish people. The two burning questions today are: Does America stand with or against Jerusalem and the nation of Israel? And, how can Believers defend Israel with prayer and spiritual warfare?

Israel is the key to America's survival. Would the events of 9/11 have happened if America had stood with Israel over the years, rather than weakening her by rewarding terrorists like Arafat and his successor, Mahmoud Abbas? The English Poet Alfred Lord Tennyson wrote: "More things are wrought by prayer than this world dreams of."[11] What might have been prevented had U.S. support for Israel been unwavering; had the churches in America banded together to pray for the peace of Jerusalem; had chosen to bless Israel?

In 1980, I interviewed Isser Harel, head of Mossad, Israeli intelligence, from 1952-1963. He informed me that terrorists would surely strike New York City's tallest building (at the time the Empire State Building). I was so convinced Harel was correct, that in 1999, I wrote a novel called *The Jerusalem Scroll* in which Osama bin Laden would obtain a nuclear bomb from the Russian mafia and attempt to blow up New York City and Los Angeles. Thank God, he never gained possession of a nuclear bomb. The United States has been blessed beyond measure, and I believe it is because she has been the world's least anti-Semitic country. But being "least" in something is not enough; the United States must become "first" in standing side-by-side with Israel and in defending God's Chosen People.

The Jewish Elders made an appeal to Jesus to come to Capernaum to the house of Cornelius, a Gentile, to heal a servant who was close to death. The Jews said to Jesus, "If anyone deserves your help, he does....for he loves the Jewish people and even built a synagogue for us."

The God of Israel pledged that He would "bless those who bless you." (Genesis 12:3, NKJV). Why Believers should wholeheartedly support the Jewish people and their beloved country, Israel, may be considered by some to be a selfish reason in some respects, but it is a valid one nonetheless. We have already seen that God's eternal covenant was passed down through Isaac, Jacob, and the twelve tribes of Israel. This means that the blessing promised by the God of Israel would come to those who particularly bless the Jewish people.

How can we bless the Jews? There are many ways this can and should be done. One of the most important and obvious ways is to support their God-given right to live in their biblical Promised Land, especially in their eternal capital city, Jerusalem. The sad fact is that many governments, international organizations, Muslim factions and even some Christian groups do not acknowledge that divine right. For Christians, this non-biblical stand weakens our testimony, weakens the nation of Israel, and weakens the United States, putting our nation in harm's way.

By contesting the right of Jews to live in their covenant land, thereby going against God's Holy Word, many are opening themselves up to be cursed! Therefore, anyone who seeks the blessings bestowed by our Heavenly Father should make sure they are obeying His command to bless His special covenant people.

The Church must never lose sight of the fact that our Lord and Savior, Jesus Christ, was born a Jew. He is the offspring of Abraham, Isaac, and King David. Believers need only look at the genealogies in Matthew and Luke. God included them in the Bible for a reason, not so we could just hurry through them or skip over them. Jesus is our King because He is David's heir to the throne. New Testament scriptures only reaffirm God's promises to Israel throughout the Old Testament.

Israel has more right to the land than any nation, having received the grant from God in a covenant with Abraham.

The great Master of the Universe reveals that our personal, family, and national welfare is closely related to how we treat the Jewish people. God not only promised to reward individuals for blessing His covenant Jewish people, but He also pledged in the same Scripture to bless families, and by extension, entire nations: "And in you all the families of the earth shall be blessed."(Genesis 12:3, NKJV) Should anyone need any other reason to support the contemporary offspring of Abraham, Isaac, and Jacob, especially in their brave endeavors to maintain a thriving modern state within biblically-designated ancestral borders?

Bulgarian pastor George Bakalav wrote of God's very special covenant with Abraham:

> Prior to Abraham, God had relationship with number of other saints such as Job and Noah. However, God promised Abraham two specific things He never promised anyone else: the land of Canaan would become the land of Israel and Abraham will have a special heir born of his own flesh and blood. This heir of Abraham would be

later recognized also as an heir of David, the promised Messiah, the Savior and the ruler of the world. Thus Abraham becomes the father of the Jewish people. The land of Israel, which at that time was occupied by the Canaanites, is given to Abraham and his decedents as part of this covenant.[12]

As we have seen, both the Old and New Testaments make abundantly clear that Christians must support Israel in every possible way. This does not mean that the Israeli people and their government are perfect. Far from it: They are fallen human beings like everyone else on Earth, in desperate need of salvation. (See II Chronicles 7:14)

While working, and praying for all Israel, we must wholeheartedly support what the sovereign Lord is doing in returning His covenant people to their God-given land. In doing so, we will be blessed as they are blessed. Best of all, we will please our Heavenly Father by obeying His revealed will on a matter that is clearly close to His heart:

> Thus says the Lord: "Against all My evil neigh-bors who touch the inheritance which I have caused My people Israel to inherit—behold,

I will pluck them out of their land and pluck
out the house of Judah from among them."
(Jeremiah 12:14, NKJV)

When we refuse to pray for the Jewish people, we
are saying simply, "God, I know better than you. I will
not obey Your Word." Almighty God has promised to
dwell with them in the land (Zechariah 2:10). God will
determine blessings or curses on America depending on
how she treats Israel. Will you join me today in blessing
Israel through prayer and intercession for her security
and the safety of her people?

PRAYER FOR ISRAEL:

Father,

You have called us to be watchmen on the walls to warn of impending attacks. Please raise up an army of intercessors for Israel. Make our duty to be watchmen on the walls of Jerusalem even more evident. As a prayer warrior, I pledge to give the Enemy no rest and no peace day or night until You establish Jerusalem and make her the praise of the earth. (See Isaiah 62:6-7) I rebuke the Enemy who comes only to steal, kill and destroy in the mighty Name of Jesus!

SCRIPTURES FOR STUDY:

Isaiah 62:6-7	Genesis 13:14-18, KJV
Genesis 17:4-8, KJV	Genesis 22:15-18, KJV
Genesis 26:1-5, KJV	Isaiah 59:19
Zechariah 9:13	Isaiah 30:19
Isaiah 62:6-7	Isaiah 45:5

3

JERUSALEM, THE HEART AND SOUL OF THE EARTH

"Yet I have chosen Jerusalem,
that My name may be there..."

2 CHRONICLES 6:6, NKJV

ALL EXPRESSIONS of Divine love still hold true for Israel today; none have been canceled. Israel—the Promised Land, Holy Land, Land of Canaan—is, and always will be, the apple of God's eye (see Zechariah 2:8). She remains God's joy and delight, His royal diadem (see Isaiah 62:3), His firstborn, His Chosen One, His beloved (see Jeremiah 2:2, Hosea 11:1). Indeed, He says of His people, "For they shall be like the jewels of a crown." (Zechariah 9:16)

Israel is not merely a long, narrow strip of land on the Mediterranean Sea; she represents only a part of the Divine land grant—from God to the descendants of Abraham, Isaac, and Jacob.

> On that day the LORD made a covenant with
> Abram and said, "To your descendants I give
> this land, from the Wadi of Egypt to the great
> river, the Euphrates—the land of the Kenites,
> Kenizzites, Kadmonites, Hittites, Perizzites,
> Rephaites, Amorites, Canaanites, Girgashites
> and Jebusites," (Genesis 15:18, NIV.)

It was a gift from Jehovah, and the ownership of Israel's land is non-negotiable. In March 2002, Senator James Inhofe (R-OK) addressed the issue of Israel's right to her land:

> Every new archeological dig supports the fact
> that the Jews have had a presence in Israel
> for 3,000 years—coins, cities, pottery, other
> cultural artifacts. The Jew's claim predates
> the claim of any other people in the region.
> The ancient Philistines are extinct as are other
> ancient peoples. They do not have the unbroken
> line the Israelis have. Ownership is and will be
> in the hands of God's Chosen People—forever.[13]

When you sign your name to a check, you represent that you possess the amount indicated on that check. God wrote His Name in Jerusalem, and He has the power and authority over that which His name represents.

On July 30, 1980, the Israeli Knesset voted to affirm a united Jerusalem as the capital of the State of Israel. Shortly afterward, I had the privilege of speaking with the man who would become my dear friend, Prime Minister Menachem Begin. We discussed the vastness of the territory held by Israel's enemies. For instance, at that time:

> Arab dictators controlled 13,486,861 square kilometers in the Middle East, and Israel controlled 20,770 (Palestinefacts.org).
>
> The population of Israel was roughly 7.8 million, compared to the population of 300 million living in the surrounding Arab countries.
>
> The odds against Israel are decidedly skewed. The Arab nations demanding a Palestinian state are represented by 21 separate countries.[14]

Several arguments have been offered as to why Palestinian Authority head, Mahmoud Abbas, continues to reject any and all offers of a Palestinian State. Chiefly, formal statehood would limit the ability of the PA and of Hamas in Gaza to commit acts of terrorism. This was a lesson learned when Gaza achieved pseudo-statehood; it became easier for Israel to retaliate when attacked. Achieving statehood would be a catastrophic move by the PA: It would lose sizeable donations from U.S., EU, and Arab backers. Would that those organizations, including the UN and Russia come to understand that the Palestinians do not want a state. It would rob them of the cover they now enjoy when it comes to terroristic acts against the Jewish people in Israel. It is obvious, when at some point in each round of negotiations the Palestinians cry foul, pick up their marbles and go home.

To this day, the same countries trying to foist a Palestinian state off on Israel do not recognize Jerusalem as the capital of Israel. The Holy City is the symbol of all that Israel represents in our world. Teddy Kollek, Jerusalem's first mayor wrote:

> Jerusalem, this beautiful, golden city, is the heart and soul of the Jewish people. One cannot live without a heart and soul. If you want one single word to symbolize all of Jewish history, that word is Jerusalem.[15]

Out of the interminable negotiations to establish a

Jewish homeland a friendship grew between Dr. Chaim Weizmann, a Jewish statesman, and Lord Balfour, the British foreign secretary. Balfour was unable to understand why the Jews were insisting that they would only accept Palestine as their permanent homeland. One day, Lord Balfour asked Dr. Weizmann for an explanation. "Mr. Balfour, let's suppose I propose that you replace London with Paris, would you accept?" A surprised Balfour responded, "But, London is ours!" Replied Weizmann, "Jerusalem was ours when London was still a swampland."[16]

The very name of the Holy City evokes a stirring in the heart and soul of both Jew and Christian. It has been called by many names: City of God, City of David, Zion, the City of the Great King, Ariel (Lion of God), Moriah (chosen of the Lord). But only one name resonates down through the centuries—Jerusalem! David's city!

A world map drawn in 1581 features Jerusalem at its very center with the then-known continents of the world surrounding it. It resembles a ship's propeller with the shaft in the center being Jerusalem. Another analogy is of Jerusalem as the navel of the earth. Its history can be summed up in one word—troubled! Lying as it does between the rival empires of Egypt to the south and

Syria to the north, both striving for dominance in the region, Israel has repeatedly been trampled by opposing armies. She has been conquered at various times by the Canaanites, Jebusites, Babylonians, Assyrians, Persians, Romans, Byzantines, Arabs, Crusaders, Ottomans, and the British. While her origins are lost in the hazy mists of antiquity, ample archaeological evidence of human habitation goes back some 4,000 years.

In *Jerusalem, Sacred City of Mankind*, Teddy Kollek and Moshe Pearlman wrote:

> The history of Jerusalem from earliest times is the history of man, a history of war and peace, of greatness and misery, of splendor and squalor, of lofty wisdom and of blood flowing in the gutters. But the golden thread, the consistent theme running through that history, is the unshakeable association of the Jewish people with the city.
>
> The story of this association is repeatedly interrupted by a succession of conquerors— Egyptians, Assyrians, Babylonians, Persians, Seleucids, Romans, Moslem Arabs, Seljuks, Crusaders, Saracens, Mamelukes, and Ottomans. Yet throughout the three thousand years since

David made it the seat of Israel's authority, the spiritual attachment of the Jews to Jerusalem has remained unbroken. It is a unique attachment.[17]

Peace reigned in Daniel's life; he was no "secret servant." God had been faithful to him, and he had no reason to doubt. Either he would be preserved in the lions' den, or not, but Daniel was committed to doing the will of God. Daniel knelt in his window in open view of passersby, his face toward the Holy City, according to 1 Kings 8:47–49 (NLT):

> But in that land of exile, they might turn to you in repentance and pray, "We have sinned, done evil, and acted wickedly." If they turn to you with their whole heart and soul in the land of their enemies and pray toward the land you gave to their ancestors—toward this city you have chosen, and toward this Temple I have built to honor your name—then hear their prayers and their petition from heaven where you live, and uphold their cause.

Seeing Daniel in earnest prayer, the instigators smugly and triumphantly scurried to the king:

> Have you not signed a decree that every man
> who petitions any god or man within thirty
> days, except you, O king, shall be cast into the
> den of lions? . . . That Daniel, who is one of the
> captives from Judah, does not show due regard
> for you, O king, or for the decree that you have
> signed, but makes his petition three times a day.
> (Daniel 6:12, 13, NKJV)

This combination of envy and enmity produced exultation from those who had devised the plan. The trap had been set, and Daniel had fallen into it; enemy vanquished—or so they thought.

The king likely felt as though he had been hit with a left hook to the jaw! He was stunned by this turn of events: A man he greatly admired was now in dire straits because of Darius' egotism.

Daniel was quickly arrested and led to the lair where the lions were confined and flung inside. Let me assure you, these were not cute little lion cubs, nor were there only one or two in the den. There were a sufficient number of lions to rip Daniel to shreds and devour him in a matter of minutes.

Darius then sealed the covering with his signet ring and returned to the palace. So distressed was the king that he spent the night wordlessly fasting. In his sleeplessness he failed to summon the musicians, or the dancing girls, or indulge in other diversions. The Bible says, "And he could not sleep." I believe he spent the night pacing in his bedchamber. At the earliest opportunity, he burst forth from his room and went in search of an answer:

> At the first light of dawn, the king got up and hurried to the lions' den. When he came near the den, he called to Daniel in an anguished voice, "Daniel, servant of the living God, has your God, whom you serve continually, been able to rescue you from the lions?" Daniel answered, "May the king live forever! My God sent his angel, and he shut the mouths of the lions. They have not hurt me, because I was found innocent in his sight. Nor have I ever done any wrong before you, Your Majesty." (Daniel 6:19–22 NIV)

It seems that every seed Daniel had sown into the king's life erupted at the mouth of the lions' den in Darius' question. He wanted to know if everything Daniel had said to him was true. Could the living God deliver, do the miraculous, save the endangered? Daniel could have echoed the words of the young son of a friend of mine and exclaimed, "That was one scary sleepover!" But he chose instead to cry out joyously, "My God sent His angel, and he shut the mouths of the lions."

There is no record that Daniel offered any argument to the king before he was led away to the lions' den; only after God had vindicated him and saved him from the jaws of the ferocious beasts did he offer any defense. He knew he had been innocent of anything other than obedience to Jehovah-Shalom, the God who was Daniel's peace in the midst of the ravening lions. Daniel had sought the kingdom of God and had been rewarded.

Daniel's prayers prevailed in the midst of Israel's captivity in Babylon and beyond:

> For thus saith the LORD, That after seventy years be accomplished at Babylon I will visit you, and perform my good word toward you, in causing you to return to this place. For I know the thoughts that I think toward you, saith the LORD, thoughts of peace, and not of evil, to give you an expected end. Then shall ye call upon me, **and ye shall go and pray unto me, and I will hearken unto you**. And ye shall

seek me, and find me, when ye shall search for me with all your heart. And I will be found of you, saith the LORD: and I will turn away your captivity, **and I will gather you from all the nations**, and from all the places whither I have driven you, saith the LORD; and I will bring you again into the place whence I caused you to be carried away captive. (Emphasis mine, Jeremiah 29:10-14, KJV)

When the Jews were driven from their land at various times, wherever they found themselves in exile, they faced toward Jerusalem when praying. Jewish synagogues faced toward Jerusalem. When a Jew built a house, part of a wall was left unfinished to symbolize that it was only a temporary dwelling—until he could return to his permanent home, Jerusalem. Even today the traditional smashing of a glass during a wedding ceremony has its roots in the Temple in Jerusalem. This act of remembering the loss of the center of Jewish festivities during the marriage feast sets "Jerusalem above [their] highest joy," (Psalm 137:6, KJV.)

Jerusalem belongs to God despite the detractors who wish to offer the city up as appeasement to her avowed enemies. Satan would dance gleefully should Israel be forced to make that move. When the Messiah returns, it will be to the City of David, not to al Quds (the Arabic name for Jerusalem.) This is only one reason why Believers need to take a stand against the Enemy and shout, "Satan, You can't have Israel!"

PRAYER FOR ISRAEL:

I come before Your throne and I bind every principality and power that is trying to destroy Israel, the land of Your people. I love the Jewish people and their homeland. Israel was born through intercession, prayer, sacrifice and biblical principles. We cry out as the Psalmist did: "Will You not revive us again, That Your people may rejoice in You?" Father, I pray that every demonic spirit will be bound in the mighty name of the Lord, and that You would pour out a river of healing upon Your land, Precious Father.

SCRIPTURES FOR STUDY:

Leviticus 25:23	Deuteronomy 32:43
Joel 2:18	2 Chronicles 7:20
Psalm 85:1-2	Jeremiah 2:7
Joel 3:1	Ezekiel 38:16
Zechariah 9:16	Genesis 17:7-8

4

JERUSALEM'S SPIRITUAL SIGNIFICANCE

Break forth together into singing, you waste
places of Jerusalem; for the LORD has comforted
his people, he has redeemed Jerusalem.

ISAIAH 52:9, RSV

WHEN COMPARED WITH the great cities of the world, Jerusalem is small in size and population. It lies beside no great river as do London, Paris, and Rome. It boasts no port, no key industries, no mineral wealth or even an adequate water supply. The city doesn't stand next to a major thoroughfare connected to the rest of the world. Why then is Jerusalem the navel of the earth, the shaft that propels the world ever forward? And why is it so often in the crosshairs of Satan's attacks?

The answer can only be found in its spiritual significance. Jerusalem is the home of two of the world's monotheistic faiths—Judaism and Christianity, and is claimed by a third—Islam. Biblical prophets proclaimed that from Jerusalem the Word of the Lord would go out to the world—a Word, which would change the moral standards of all mankind:

> For out of Zion shall go the law, and the word
> of the LORD from Jerusalem. (Isaiah 2:3, ESV)

The spiritual stature of Jerusalem is echoed in its physical situation; it sits atop the Judean hills high above the surrounding countryside. Traveling to Jerusalem is always spoken of as "going up to Jerusalem." Those who leave the City of God are said to go down—in perhaps more than just the physical sense.

When viewing the history of Jerusalem as a whole, no other city has suffered as has David's City. At times the city has been overrun by violent assailants. It is recorded in Jeremiah that the city would surrender after suffering the horrors of starvation—and be reduced to cannibalism (see Jeremiah 19).

While Christian and Muslim claims to Jerusalem came much later, the chronicle of the Jews in Jerusalem began three millennia ago, and has never ceased. The link of the Jewish people has been historical, religious, cultural, physical, and fundamental. It has never been voluntarily broken; any absence of Jews from their beloved city has been the result of foreign persecution and expulsion. To the Jews alone belongs David's City, the City of God.

For the Jewish people whose cry for centuries has been, "Next year Jerusalem," it is more than a location on the map, it is not just a tourist stop where one can visit various holy sites; Jerusalem *is* holy. It is the essence of that for which Jews have hoped and prayed and cried and died. It is their God-given land.

The God who cannot lie made a vow to His people:

> The LORD had said to David and to Solomon his son, "In this house and in Jerusalem, which I have chosen out of all the tribes of Israel, I will put My name forever." (2 Kings 21:7)

Israel is *God's* Dream; the title deed belongs to Him. It is His to bestow on whomever He will—and He has given the right of occupation to the Jewish people. When God made His eternal promises to Israel, there was no United Nations, no United States, no Russia, no European Union, and no Arab League; there were only pagan nations to challenge this dream, to challenge God and His Word. Today, those pagan voices are challenging the right of the Jews to occupy a unified Jerusalem.

When you and I as Christians are apathetic toward God's Divine plan or His eternal purpose, it means that we are rejecting our Lord's assignment to the Church. God's prophetic time clock has been set on Jerusalem time throughout history, and the spotlight of heaven remains shining upon the Jews as His Chosen People. It began with them, and it will end with them.

We embrace the name of Christ and serve the God of Abraham, Isaac, and Jacob and find strength. We heed the warnings of the prophets Isaiah, Jeremiah, Ezekiel, Daniel, Hosea, and Joel and find direction. We sing the Psalms of King David and find hope. The mention of Jerusalem quickens our hearts, for it is our spiritual city. We, then, must join our Jewish brothers and sisters in their fight against anti-Semitism and the threat of terrorism and reap the blessings of God.

God's plan is an eternal one! As Christians, we cannot afford to neglect our responsibility to stand with the House of Israel. It is as important as it is to believe the promises of God. As Christians, we are the engrafted vine; we bow before a Jewish Messiah; and what we do matters in the light of eternity.

Jerusalem is the only city for which God commands us to pray. When you pray for Jerusalem as instructed in Psalm 122:6, you are not praying for stones or dirt, you are praying for revival (2 Chronicles 7:14), and for the Lord's return. Also, you are joining our Lord, the Good Samaritan, in His ministry of love and comfort to the suffering House of Israel:

> "Inasmuch as you did it to one of the least of these My brethren, you did it to Me." (Matthew 25:40, NKJV)

This is our divine commission.

King David explained precisely why God Almighty has commanded us to pray for the peace of Jerusalem, and has commanded a blessing upon us for doing so. This revelation is found in Psalm 122:8: "For the sake of my brethren and companions, I will now say, 'Peace be within you.'" God is telling us to pray for the peace of the inhabitants of Jerusalem. David felt that prayer needed to be offered up for all of his brothers and friends who lived there. Prayer needs to be offered today for the Children of

Israel and for peace for those who reside there from the over 120 nations of the world. It is the city most targeted by terrorists, simply because of hatred for the Jewish people and the significance of Jerusalem. It has drawn the Jewish people of the world like a prophetic magnet—those who have prayed, "Next year in Jerusalem."

In Psalm 122:9, David's revelation says, "Because of the house of the LORD our God I will seek your good." When we pray for the peace of Jerusalem, we are ultimately praying for Satan to be bound. In Isaiah 14, Satan said he would battle God from the Temple of the Lord, on the sides of the north:

> For you have said in your heart: 'I will ascend into heaven, I will exalt my throne above the stars of God; I will also sit on the mount of the congregation On the farthest sides of the north. (Isaiah 14:13, NKJV)

When we pray for the peace of Jerusalem, we are praying for those who live there, and we are praying for the Messiah to return. The prophecies of the Bible point to the Temple of the Lord as the key flashpoint that will bring the nations of the world to Jerusalem, resulting in the battle that will end Satan's reign over the earth for all eternity. It will spell his final defeat!

In 691 A.D., Islamic adherents of the Umayyad dynasty began a campaign to "exalt and glorify"[18] the city of Jerusalem. Umayyad Caliph Abd al-Malik built the Dome of the Rock over the Foundation Stone, the Holy of Holies. It was thought to have been erected in direct competition with Christianity. The edifice still stands today. Islam later attributed another event to the Foundation Stone: the binding of the son of Abraham the "Hanif," the first Monotheist. As the Koran does not explicitly mention the name Isaac, Muslim commentators have erroneously identified the son bound by Abraham as Ishmael. Thus Islam teaches that the title deed to Jerusalem and the Temple Mount and all of Israel belongs to the Arabs—not the Jews.

In fact, Mohammed never set foot in Jerusalem, nor is the city mentioned by name in the Koran. His only connection to Jerusalem was through his dream or vision where he found himself in a "temple that is most remote" (Koran, Sura). It was not until the 7th Century that Muslim adherents decided to identify the "temple most remote" as a mosque in Jerusalem (perhaps for political reasons).

The truth remains that this site on which now stands the Dome of the Rock, and is sacred to Jews as the Temple site, will be the basis for the battle of the ages that will one day be fought.

There is a divine reason the Church was born in Zion. As was the case then, and still is today, all roads lead to Jerusalem, Judea, and Samaria. Heaven and Earth met in Jerusalem, and will, when Messiah returns, meet there again. The destiny of America and the world is linked to Jerusalem. It is the epicenter of spiritual warfare and will affect the entire world.

Jerusalem, Judea, and Samaria are the battle zones. It is no accident that the Great Commission is directed toward these prophetic areas:

> But ye shall receive power, after that the Holy Ghost is come upon you: and ye shall be witnesses unto me both in Jerusalem, and in all Judaea, and in Samaria, and unto the uttermost part of the earth. (Acts 1:8, KJV)

If Christians are not salt and light, then the Great Commission will become the Great Omission!

If our Lord and Savior reached out in compassion to

Israel, and made prayer for her His highest priority, do we dare make it our lowest? There is a direct correlation between the power that Heaven promised for the Church at its birth in Jerusalem, and the Church's obedience to be a witness in Jerusalem, Judea, and Samaria. The Church cannot, and must not, ignore Christ's eternal mission for her, and at the same time, expect power from on high. If His disciples' obedience was directly related to a power surge from Heaven and the birth of the Church, can disobedience empower the Church and lift her heavenward to fulfill her final mission?

Another significant reason why you and I as Believers should rejoice in Israel's physical restoration and strongly support her continued existence in the Middle East is the prophesied future of her ancient and modern capital city, Jerusalem. Holy Writ reveals that Zion is to be the very seat of the Messiah's earthly reign. All the nations on earth will come up to visit Jerusalem when Jesus rules from the Holy City as King of Kings and Lord of Lords!

It is clearly evident from Scripture that the Sovereign Lord of Creation has chosen the city of Jerusalem as His earthly capital. This was decreed by the very same God who promised to restore His covenanted Jewish people to the sacred city and surrounding land in the last days before the Second Coming. How can Christians look for and welcome Jesus' prophesied return, and not rejoice in and actively defend the Jewish return that was foretold to at least partially precede it?

God has never revoked Abraham's title deed to the land, nor has He given it to anyone else. The spot where God confirmed His covenant is an area north of Jerusalem between Bethel and Ai. It is in the heart of what is called the West Bank, or Judea and Samaria. (The United Nations refers to this as "occupied territory," and demands that Israel relinquish it.) An inalienable right is one that cannot be given away. The Bible declares this to be so in Genesis 25:23. The people were forbidden to sell the land because, "The land must not be sold permanently, because the land is mine and you are but aliens and my tenants." (NKJV)

Jerusalem is the only city God claims as His own; it is called the City of God and the Holy City in Scripture. He declared to Solomon in 2 Chronicles 33:7:

> In this house and in Jerusalem, which I have chosen out of all the tribes of Israel, I will put my Name forever, (NKJV.)

To this day, America's leaders refuse to recognize Jerusalem as Israel's capital. This is a grave mistake. I have shouted the words of Prime Minister Menachem Begin as a warning from the White House in Washington to the Royal Palace in Madrid as I rebuked world leaders with his words, "God does not recognize America's non-recognition position!" Nor will He countenance Satan's attempts to hijack what belongs solely to Him.

PRAYER FOR ISRAEL:

God be merciful to Israel; bless her, and cause Your face to shine upon her, that Your way may be known on earth, and Your salvation among all nations. Let the peoples praise You, O God; Let all the peoples praise You. Oh, let the nations be glad and sing for joy! For You shall judge the people righteously, and govern the nations on earth. Let the peoples praise You, O God; let all the peoples praise You. Then the earth will yield her increase; and God, our own God, shall bless us. He shall bless us, and all the ends of the earth shall fear Him.   Psalm 67

SCRIPTURES FOR STUDY:

Isaiah 60:1-3	Isaiah 2:2-4
Isaiah 33:20	Zechariah 8:3
Psalm 132:4-5	2 Samuel 7:10
Isaiah 11:12	Joel 3:16
Psalm 125:1-2	Zechariah 2:5, 8

5

GOD'S WORD IS
IMMUTABLE

For out of Zion shall go forth the law,
And the word of the Lord from Jerusalem.

ISAIAH 2:3, NASB

AS WE HAVE SEEN, the survival of the Jews is a fulfillment of biblical prophecy. Had the Jews not survived, God's Word would not be true! Throughout the Bible God made eternal promises to the people of Israel, some of which He has yet to fulfill.

God made a covenant with the Children of Israel and deeded the land to Abraham, Isaac, and Jacob through their descendants—not through Ishmael and his descendants. His covenant promise cannot be broken—not by the Jews' captivity in other nations, not by war, not by repeated cycles of iniquity and penitence. Ultimately His chosen ones return to their land of promise—not because of mandates issued by other countries or the United Nations; it is God's covenant promise fulfilled.

Throughout the centuries, a remnant—God's precious seed—has always remained in the Promised Land. That you and I live today to see the scattered Jews brought back and restored to their covenant land should be a matter of both wonder and worship for a God who keeps His promises—always:

> . . . for the LORD is good and his gracious love stands forever. His faithfulness remains from generation to generation. (Psalm 100:5, ISV)

The return of the Jews to the Promised Land following World War II required the Christian Church to take a closer look at the Abrahamic covenant because of the revulsion of the Holocaust. It was a combination of the return and the awfulness of what had been done to the Jewish people in the concentration camps that dealt a death blow to anti-Semitism in many, but sadly, not all churches.

Christians cannot choose to believe John 3:16 but disavow scriptures that call us to support His Chosen

People. We must either believe the entire Bible, or none of it. Israel is the fulfillment of biblical prophecy. To purposefully close our eyes to the cries of His people is like willfully and disdainfully ignoring God's instructions in His Word. The fact that the Jewish people exist is a miracle. The rebirth of the Nation of Israel is a miracle. The restoration of the Hebrew language is a miracle, as is the return of the Jewish people to their homeland, and the reunification of Jerusalem.

You either embrace Israel or you oppose Israel. One cannot straddle the fence; it's just that simple. Why do we as Christians aid Israel? Because God affirms Israel in His Word. I have heard some Christians say disdainfully, "I will not support the Jews in Israel. They are sinners, and the nation is a sinful one." How easily we forget the countless mercies God has shown to a sinful United States to whom He made not one direct promise. How can we sing, "God Bless America," when this nation leads the world in having murdered a number approaching 60 million babies by abortion since Roe vs. Wade became law—and then curse Israel with a self-righteous attitude? When you do the math, that is approximately the number of total casualties of the Holocaust and World War II combined.

Given that Germany faced judgment for its actions in the war, how, then shall the United States escape judgment? Will turning away from Israel be the straw that breaks the camel's back? And if yes, what then awaits America?

True, some Jews are guilty of the same sins as other secular Western nations—abortion, homosexuality, murder, adultery, and more. However, the promises of God given to the Children of Israel through the Old Testament prophets were unconditional. Fulfillment of His prophetical edicts is not reliant upon their belief, submission, or uprightness; it is entirely dependent on God's supreme power and His unchangeable resolve (Isaiah 2:2-5). He promised that after His people were returned to Israel, He would be revealed to them:

> Therefore say: This is what the Sovereign LORD says: "Although I sent them far away among the nations and scattered them among the countries, yet for a little while I have been a sanctuary for them in the countries where they have gone." Therefore say: "This is what the Sovereign LORD says: 'I will gather you from the nations and bring you back from the countries where you have been scattered, and I will give you back the

land of Israel again.' "They will return to it and remove all its vile images and detestable idols. I will give them an undivided heart and put a new spirit in them; I will remove from them their heart of stone and give them a heart of flesh. Then they will follow my decrees and be careful to keep my laws. They will be my people, and I will be their God." Jeremiah 11:1-20, NIV)

It is our responsibility as Christians to pray with and for the Jewish people. Those who stand in opposition to Israel are not merely anti-Semitic. The battle is not simply a physical one; it is spiritual. The powers behind it can only be defeated through intercessory prayer and through love for those God loves.

John, the brother of Jesus Christ, wrote:

If someone says, "I love God," and hates his brother, he is a liar; for the one who does not love his brother whom he has seen, cannot love God whom he has not seen. (I John 4:20, RSV)

To summarize the 66 books of the Bible in one word, you only have to say "Israel." The Bible begins with and ends with Israel. There is no word used more. There are no promises given to any people more than to Israel. Israel's very existence demonstrates the faithfulness of God, the inspiration and infallibility of the Bible, and the sovereignty of God.

Today, there is a doctrine in vogue spawned in Hell, which teaches that the Church has replaced Israel in the plans and heart of God. This doctrine is known alternately as replacement theology, progressive dispensationalism, or supersessionism. The early Church did not teach this; its roots date back to the European Church. This patently false doctrine states that the Church has supplanted Israel in God's plan for the ages, and that the Jews have been rejected; that they have been blinded for having crucified Christ. These followers believe Israel failed God and as a result was replaced by the Church. It teaches that the Church is a spiritual Israel and that Jerusalem is any town in which there is a church.

The prevailing view among those espousing supersessionism—that the Church has replaced God's Chosen People—is vastly different from the theology taught in the New Testament. The Church is totally divergent from Israel—the two are not interchangeable. The Church was born on the day of Pentecost; Israel was born of God's covenant with Abraham.

For centuries the evils of replacement theology have resembled a cancer within the Body of Christ. The claim that the Jews rejected Christ, therefore all the promises of Abraham were bestowed on the Church and all the curses fell upon Israel is a patent error. In recent years, Evangelical Christians have worked diligently to dispel that lie.

How do you know if your own church believes in replacement theology or supersessionism? Simply put, if the Church does not support Israel or the Jewish people, there is a strong possibility that it is because of this doctrine. Many churches will not acknowledge 1) that they teach this philosophy, and 2) that it is even believed. Israel is the litmus test.

In the first place, replacement theology rejects the concept that the promises God made to Israel are for this present hour; that instead, they were cancelled at Calvary. Ergo, these promises now fall to the Church, which has replaced Israel. The absurdity of this theology is that if Christian leaders believe God ended His covenant with the Jewish people, they must also believe He might revoke His promises to them as well!

What exactly do these supersessionists believe?

- ✧ They tend to be anti-Israel, and therefore do not honor Israel.

- ✧ They tend to be pro-Palestinian.

- ✧ They marginalize Christians who support Israel, even with humanitarian issues.

Obviously, these theologians have abandoned the apostle Paul's teaching to the Romans. He wrote:

> I say then, has God cast away His people? Certainly not! For I also am an Israelite, of the seed of Abraham, of the tribe of Benjamin. God has not cast away His people whom He foreknew. Or do you not know what the Scripture says of Elijah, how he pleads with God against Israel? (Romans 11:1-2, NKJV)

Replacement theology was first developed by Justin Martyr (circa 100–165 AD) and Irenaeus of Lyon (circa 130–200 AD). It was widely accepted within the Church by the fourth century. It has led to a great deal of persecution of Jews by Christians. Although the Catholic Church officially reversed its stance on replacement theology in the twentieth century, many conservative Protestant groups still believe in this doctrine.

Pastor and author Dr. John MacArthur said of the fallacy that Israel had been abandoned:

> God forbid that we should boast. If a Gentile boasts, that is being ridiculous. That is absurd because you're not giving life to the root [Israel]; the root's giving life to you. You're only a branch. You owe everything to the covenant God made with Israel. Keep Israel in the right perspective.[19]

To believe that God broke His covenant with Israel is heresy. You would have to accuse God Almighty of being a promise breaker! Do you believe God broke His covenant with Abraham, Isaac, or Jacob, and by extension that He might break His covenant with you?

When the Church tries to replace Israel:

✦ Arrogance and egotism replace love and compassion.

- It becomes boastful and complacent.

- Both Israel and the Jewish people are diminished.

- Anti-Semitism becomes rampant.

- Bible prophecies lose their importance and fulfillment is often overlooked.

- The Old Testament loses its significance and substance. The Bible of the early Church was not the New Testament, but rather the Hebrew Scriptures.

Sadly, the Church failed from its inception to realize the importance of those truths. Had that not been the case, the anti-Semitism that has plagued it for centuries might have been circumvented. Instead, the Church has been infected with the cancer of replacement theology—a very real violation of the Word of God. It has often made the Church a repository of hatred rather than love as it should have been for the past 2000 years.

In Numbers 23:19, ESV, we are told of God's infallibility:

God is not man, that he should lie, or a son of

man, that he should change his mind. Has he
said, and will he not do it? Or has he spoken,
and will he not fulfill it?

Hebrews 6:18 tells us it is *impossible* for God to lie; and
Titus 1:2 states flatly that God *cannot* lie.

If a God who does not and cannot lie made a covenant
with the Jewish people, He *will* keep His word.

PRAYER FOR ISRAEL:
(BASED ON PSALM 140:1-8)

Jehovah God,

Rescue Israel from evildoers; protect her from the violent, who devise evil plans in their hearts and stir up war every day. They make their tongues as sharp as a serpent's; the poison of vipers is on their lips. Keep Israel safe, LORD, from the hands of the wicked; protect me from the violent, who devise ways to trip her feet. The arrogant have hidden a snare for Israel; they have spread out the cords of their net and have set traps for Your Chosen People along their path. I say to the LORD, "You are the God of Israel." Hear, LORD, my cry for mercy for the nation of Israel. Sovereign LORD, my strong deliverer, shield Israel in the day of battle. Do not grant the wicked their desires, LORD; do not let their plans succeed. (Paraphrased)

SCRIPTURES FOR STUDY:

Romans 11:1-2	Isaiah 2:2-5
Jeremiah 23:7-8	Ezekiel 11:16-20
Amos 9:13-15	Zechariah 8:1-8
Psalm 140	Psalm 20
Jeremiah 31:7	Genesis 35:10-12

6

SALVATION IS OF THE JEWS

*"The LORD lives; and blessed be my rock, and
exalted be my God, the rock of my salvation. . .*

II SAMUEL 22:47, RSV

ANOTHER COMPELLING REASON for Christians
everywhere to enthusiastically intercede for the Jewish
people is this: Our eternal salvation has come through the
agency of the Jews. The physical descendants of Jacob
wrote all but a small portion of the Bible, the world's
bestselling book. The Bible says:

> For if the Gentiles have shared in the Jews'
> spiritual blessings, they owe it to the Jews
> to share with them their material blessings.
> (Romans 15:27, NIV)

Christians owe a debt of eternal gratitude to the Jewish
people for their contributions that gave birth to our faith.

As Christians, we are also indebted to the lineage of the Jewish people for our Lord and Savior Jesus Christ and to the conservation of the Holy Scriptures.

Both the *Tanakh* (Jewish Bible) and the Christian New Testament disclose that of all the nations on the earth only one was ordained by God to be saved: Israel. The Messiah was to be born in Bethlehem, be taken to Egypt for His preservation, grow up in Nazareth, ride into Jerusalem on the foal of an ass, and there stand in judgment. He would then give His life freely for the sins of all mankind.

I have heard it said, "The reason I don't support Israel is because the Jews crucified Christ. They are under judgment because they rejected God's Word." The truth is that although men were the instruments of death, no one forced Christ to die. John 10:17 tells us that Christ willingly gave His life:

> Therefore My Father loves Me, because I lay down My life that I may take it again. No one takes it from Me, but I lay it down of Myself. I have power to lay it down, and I have power to take it again. (John 10:17-18, NASV)

Dr. Billy Graham wrote:

> Jesus actually had avoided capture or death at
> the hands of His enemies on several occasions,
> but as He approached Jerusalem for the last
> time He knew His work was almost finished.
> "My appointed time is near," He said shortly
> before His arrest (see Matthew 26:18). Why did
> He not escape? The reason is because He knew
> God had sent Him into the world for one reason:
> To become the complete and final sacrifice for
> our sins. This could only be accomplished if He
> endured the judgment and death we all deserve
> for our sins—and this is exactly what happened
> when He went to the cross.[20]

From the moment God made a covenant with Abraham,
his offspring became God's Chosen People:

> For you are a people holy to the LORD your God.
> The LORD your God has chosen you out of all
> the peoples on the face of the earth to be his
> people, his treasured possession. (Deuteronomy
> 7:6, NIV)

God did not choose a people with mighty armies feared

by the surrounding nations. When He made the promise to Abraham, his tribe numbered only seventy. When the compact was sealed, Abraham had no children at all—neither Ishmael nor Isaac. Yet God continued to make promises to His friend:

> He would have as many descendants as there is dust on the earth (Genesis 13:16), as there are stars in the sky (Genesis 15:15), and as there is sand upon the seashore (Genesis 22:17; Genesis 26:4.)
>
> These descendants would occupy much territory, (Genesis 28:14.)
>
> They would become a great and mighty nation (Genesis 18:18). And not only one nation, but many nations (Genesis 17:5.)
>
> This nation would be a ruling nation; among his descendants would be kings. God promised to make him exceedingly fruitful (Genesis 17:6, and Genesis 27:29.) God has not failed to keep a single promise.

Since the establishment of the Church, some theologians seem to have adopted the erroneous philosophy that God has forsaken His Chosen People. Nothing could be further from the truth; God will never forsake either the land or His people. (See Isaiah 45:17 and Romans 11:26)

When speaking to the Samaritan woman about eternal life, Jesus pointed out that His Heavenly Father's free gift of eternal salvation has been brought to the world via the Jews, "You worship that which you do not know; we know what we worship, for **salvation is of the Jews.**" (Emphasis mine, John 4:22, ASV)

Truthfully, Jews are sometimes, but not always, hated because they are deemed to be wealthy; yet Jews of every social stratum were forced into ghettos and concentration camps. The argument that Jews are hated solely because they "crucified Christ" has never been valid. Simply, they are hated because they are Jewish. Distinguished theologian Edward H. Flannery wrote:

> It was Judaism that brought the concept of a God-given universal moral law into the world... the Jew carries the burden of God in history and for this he has never been forgiven.[21]

If the most precious gift Christians will ever possess came by means of the Jewish prophets, leaders, teachers, and in particular, Jesus the Messiah, how can we have any attitude other than one of deep gratitude toward Jacob's offspring? We who are Gentiles should be extremely thankful that God, in His shining wisdom and gracious mercy, has allowed us as "wild olive branches" to be grafted into the rich Tree of Israel, as revealed in Romans 11:17.

Satan has no problem with people following after any of the myriad man-conceived religions available in the world today. He knows they all lead to a downward path of destruction.

In his New Testament letter to the Romans, the Apostle Paul went on to point out that the "grafted in" Gentile Church does not somehow tower over the Jewish people, as many have maintained over the centuries and still do today. Rather, it is the original covenant people that remain the bedrock "root" that supports every Christian's spiritual life:

> . . . do not boast against the branches. But if you do boast, remember that you do not support the root, but the root supports you. (Romans 11:18, ISV)

Peter Wehner of *Commentary Magazine* wrote:

Israel is far from perfect—but it is, in the totality of its acts, among the most estimable and impressive nations in human history. Its achievements and moral accomplishments are staggering—which is why, in my judgment, evangelical Christians should keep faith with the Jewish state...Israel warrants support based on the here and now; on what it stands for and what it stands against and what its enemies stand for and against; and for reasons of simple justice. What is required to counteract the anti-Israel narrative and propaganda campaign is a large-scale effort at education... in a manner that tells a remarkable and moving story...

To my coreligionists I would simply point out an unpleasant truth: hatred for Israel is a burning fire throughout the world. Those of the Christian faith ought to be working to douse the flames rather than to intensify them.[22]

The truth is, God is much more merciful than Man. Lamentations 3:22, KJV states: "Through the Lord's mercies we are not consumed, Because His compassions fail not."

Perhaps the reason God has forestalled judgment is that He still has a remnant—Abraham's "ten righteous" if you will—who intercede in prayer and continue to carry the torch of righteousness in a dark and dying world. This is only one of the many reasons the Church of Jesus Christ must take up the banner of prayer and intercession and take the battle to Satan through spiritual warfare. We dare not cower in fear, but stand with God-ordained courage and roar: Satan, you can't have Israel!

PRAYER FOR ISRAEL:

Father,

Your Word says that no weapon formed against me shall prosper. I stand on that promise for Israel and for Your Chosen People. You also tell me that I dwell in the secret place of the Most High, under the shadow of the Almighty. Lord, I acknowledge You in all my ways so that You strengthen me for warfare through the power of the Holy Spirit. You have promised never to leave me or forsake me. The Psalmist David said, "For Jehovah is my refuge! I choose the God above all gods to shelter me." (Psalm 91:9, LB)

SCRIPTURES FOR STUDY:

II Chronicles 7:14	Psalm 4:8
Psalm 91:1-16	Psalm 28:7
Ezra 8:21	II Timothy 4:18
Matthew 28:20	Psalm 37:39-40
Proverbs 1:33	Proverbs 29:25
Job 28:28	

7

GOD ABHORS ANTI-SEMITISM

*"For he who touches you touches
the apple [pupil] of his Eye."*

ZECHARIAH 2:8, NASB.

Anti-Semitism is hatred against all Jews. At its very root is actually hatred of God, His Son, and His Word. You cannot love Jesus whom you have not seen (who was born a Jew) if you don't love the Jewish people whom you have seen. If you refuse to bless the House of Israel when it is in your power to do so, what evidence of true Christian love do you have to present to a Holy God?

Martin Niemoller, the anti-Nazi theologian and Lutheran pastor wrote in his poem, *First they came:*

> First they came for the Socialists,
> and I did not speak out—
> Because I was not a Socialist.

Then they came for the Trade Unionists,
and I did not speak out—
Because I was not a Trade Unionist.

Then they came for the Jews,
and I did not speak out—
Because I was not a Jew.

Then they came for me—and there
was no one left to speak for me.[23]

Hitler employed the anti-Semitic hoax, *The Protocols of the Learned Elders of Zion,* to murder six million Jews during World War II. Historian Norman Cohn suggested that Hitler used the *Protocols* as his primary justification for initiating the Holocaust—his "warrant for genocide."[24]

The trend continues today among Arab countries:

... in the Middle East, where a large number of Arab and Muslim regimes and leaders have endorsed them as authentic...The 1988 charter of Hamas, a Palestinian Islamist group, states that *The Protocols of the Elders of Zion* embodies the plan of the Zionists.[25] Recent endorsements in the 21st century have been made by the Grand Mufti of Jerusalem, Sheikh Ekrima Sa'id Sabri, the education ministry of Saudi Arabia, member of the Greek Parliament Ilias Kasidiaris, and young earth creationist and tax protester Kent Hovind.[26]

The appalling historical record reveals that Jewish people have been the target of fierce discrimination and persecution over the centuries even in so-called Christian lands. Vatican-inspired Crusaders deliberately murdered Jews during the Middle Ages. The Roman Catholic Inquisitions were directed against the Jews in Spain and elsewhere, leaving many dead or in prison. The pogroms of Russia and Eastern Europe forced Jews from their homes, and left untold numbers slaughtered.

As evil as these anti-Semitic assaults were, they all pale in comparison to the Holocaust of World War II. A full one-third of the entire Jewish race was annihilated by Hitler's Nazi forces. The utter horror of this hellish practice that was the Holocaust as revealed by the testimonies of death-camp survivors cannot be overstressed. Something to which we tend to give little credence is the definition of the term "Nazi." It is often used so randomly in this day that we forget it has an absolute meaning.

It was a term coined by the National Socialist Movement, an organization devoted solely to the most malicious and deadly form of anti-Semitism.

Too late, many Germans recognized the blessings that the Jewish people brought to their society before Hitler's tragic rise to power. Jewish composers, scientists, doctors, teachers, writers, and others contributed their significant talents and intelligence and were callously repaid in Hitler's death chambers.

In the twenty-first century, anti-Semitism continues to raise its ugly head in the unlikeliest of places:

> Belgian Justice Minister Stefaan De Clerck shocked the country's Jewish community by voicing support for an initiative to provide amnesty to Nazi collaborators during WWII, and for his suggestion that it may behoove the government to "forget" its Nazi past. During a television debate, De Clerck said that the country should not focus on the crimes it committed as it was already in the past. In fairness there are plenty of crimes being committed now against Belgium's Jews. The country's anti-Semitism is partly why the safety of European Jews is at its

lowest since the Second World War, with anti-Jewish attacks at postwar highs. So maybe De Clerck was saying that Belgians should focus on their present anti-Semitism rather than on their past anti-Semitism.[27]

Could this be, I wonder, why Belgium became the focus of the manhunt for accessories to the bloody terrorist attacks that took place in France in November 2015? The violence claimed the lives of at least 130 and wounded more than 350. In a *USA Today* article, journalist Oren Dorrell wrote, "Recruiting network Sharia4Belgium wants to convert Belgium — whose capital of Brussels is also the capital of the European Union — into an Islamic State."[28] Salah Abdeslam, the brother of one of the slain jihadists was believed to have taken refuge in Belgium.

Unfortunately some say, "I don't need to reach out to the suffering House of Israel. Why, the Bible says there will be wars and rumors of wars over there, until the Messiah comes. It's all part of prophecy." (See Matthew 24:6)

To simply say that there is no need to pray and support the Jewish people, my friend, is anti-Semitic nonsense. It is to say to Nehemiah, Esther and even our Lord that they were wrong to pray and reach out in love to the House of Israel. There are hundreds of examples of prophets, priests and pontiffs who chose to light a candle rather than curse the darkness. Jesus is our perfect example. He fed the hungry. He gave water to the thirsty. He healed the sick. He was not afraid to deliver the truth to the skeptics of His day. He also prophesied that the Temple would be torn down, with Jerusalem left in shambles.

The Bible says the same thing about the entire world in 2 Timothy 3:1, KJV, "But know this, that in the last days perilous times will come."

And in Matthew 24:6-8, KJV:

> And you will hear of wars and rumors of wars. See that you are not troubled; for all these things must come to pass, but the end is not yet. For nation will rise against nation, and kingdom against kingdom. And there will be famines, pestilences, and earthquakes in various places. All these are the beginning of sorrows.

If we are to do nothing for the Jewish people because they do not embrace Jesus Christ, then why do we do everything in our power to help hurting unbelievers in other lands? If we are to do nothing, then why did the Psalmist say in chapter 122, verse 6, NKJV: "Pray for the peace of Jerusalem. May they prosper who love you." The time has come to stand up and be counted. Also in Psalm 122:9, we are charged to "seek what is best for you, O Jerusalem." (NLT) It is time to ask, seek, and knock for Israel's good:

> Ask and it will be given to you; seek and you will find; knock and the door will be opened to you. For everyone who asks receives; the one who seeks finds; and to the one who knocks, the door will be opened. (Matthew 7:7, NIV)

The Apostle Paul warned Christians not to behave arrogantly toward the physical descendants of Jacob. However, arrogance would have been welcomed in comparison to the ugly hatred and deadly violence that has frequently been aimed at the Jewish people in the name of Christ. This alone should be reason enough for contemporary Christians to sincerely intercede in prayer for the Jewish people and for the land of Israel.

PRAYER FOR ISRAEL:

Father,

I love the Jewish people and the land of Israel. In the Bible You declare, "Call to me and I will answer you and show you great and mighty things which you do not know." (Jeremiah 33:3) I call unto You right now for your Chosen People. I ask You to pour out Your Holy Spirit on their land. In the mighty name of Jesus, I bind principalities and powers and spiritual wickedness in high places. I declare that Jesus is Lord over Israel. I pray that the weapons available to me through the power of prayer will be mighty, pulling down the strongholds over Israel. In Jesus name!

SCRIPTURES FOR STUDY:

Ephesians 3:10	Psalm 122:1
Matthew 16:17	Ephesians 1:22
Hebrews 10:25	Colossians 1:18
Acts 20:28	Acts 12:5
Ephesians 3:21	I Timothy 3:15

8

COMFORT ISRAEL

*"Comfort ye, comfort ye my people saith your God.
Speak ye comfortably to Jerusalem. . . "*

ISAIAH 40:1-2, KJV

THE SETTING of Isaiah 40 follows the dispersion of
the Jewish people to Babylon. The Children of Israel had
been captives, distraught by the circumstances in which
they found themselves. Those left behind in Jerusalem,
ruled too by the Babylonians, were equally distressed.
As a release for their grief and agitation, the book of
Lamentations was written. In Lamentations 1:17, NLT,
the writer records, "Jerusalem reaches out for help, but
no one comforts her."

Now in Isaiah 40, change has come: "Comfort, oh
comfort my people. . . Speak kindly to Jerusalem." (Isaiah
40:1-2, NASB) The Hebrew people have paid the price for

their sin and the time for comfort has come. Professor and theologian John Goldingay wrote of the time:

> The city [of Jerusalem] is like a woman who has lost husband and children and sits desolate like Job on his heap of ashes. She has sat this way for nearly half a century. Now a voice declares Comfort, comfort my people. The time for the plaint in Lamentations is over. And the one who speaks is **your God**.[29]

The voice heard is not just any voice; it is God's voice. The price has been paid and comfort has come as a result of Israel's repentance, of sighing and lamenting over the cause of their captivity. Jehovah, merciful and gracious, has now sent His spokesman to offer comfort and consolation. He has sent a servant to offer tenderness, the balm of Gilead to bind up their wounded spirits and broken hearts. God's response to their repentance is "I am with you. I have neither forgotten nor forsaken you." That theme is repeated again and again throughout the remainder of the Book of Isaiah.

The children of Israel had suffered through a terrible calamity. They were in need of comfort, of being assured that their time of catastrophe was coming to an end. It was time for encouragement, for knowing that God had not forsaken them. Darkness had covered the land, but Israel had not been cast aside by Yahweh. The time for restoration was at hand; the time for comfort had come. The God of all comfort had declared it to be a time for consolation.

In his commentary on Isaiah, Old Testament scholar Walter Brueggemann writes:

> Enough! Enough sentence, enough penalty, enough payment, enough exile, enough displacement! This is an assertion of forgiveness, but it is not cheap or soft or easy forgiveness. There is, in any case, a limit to the sentence. It can be satisfied and served out. And now it is ended![30]

The prophetic word given by Isaiah was not just for that time, it is a God-given mandate to Christians today to offer comfort, encouragement, and emotional and financial support to the suffering House of Israel. If this Scripture is not for Christians, then for whom is it? Nation after nation has turned its back on the Jewish people. God will not forget those who abandon Israel, just as He will not forget those who reach out in love and assistance. This assignment is echoed in Paul's second letter to the Corinthians:

> Praise be to the God and Father of our Lord Jesus Christ, the Father of compassion and the God of all comfort, who comforts us in all our troubles, so that we can comfort those in any trouble with the comfort we ourselves receive from God. (II Corinthians 1:3-4, NIV)

If you and I are to be godly, if our major focus is to become more like Christ, we must offer comfort and consolation to God's chosen people. In Isaiah 6:8, NKJV, God called out, "Whom shall I send, and who will go for us?" Isaiah cried, "Here am I; send me." The Lord is saying that praying Christians can win the war being fought right now in the land of the Bible. Wake up, mighty men; wake up, mighty women! Wake up Esthers and Nehemiahs!

The House of Israel seems to have fallen among robbers who have not only stolen their land but their lives. Many people watch with little, if any, concern as Jews again become scapegoats for the world's inequities. The economy tanks—must be the fault of Jewish bankers. Disease runs rampant—must have been caused by the Jews. Floods, fires, hurricanes, tornadoes, famine—the Jews have to be somehow responsible. Right? That has certainly been the mindset of Arab leaders for decades.

According to an article in the *Jerusalem Post*, there are as many reasons Arabic-speaking people believe these lies as there are Arabs in the region:

> ...A Swiss reporter interviewed a high-ranking official in the oil-rich United Arab Emirates and asked why the school system wasn't better. Ah, explained the man, this was all due to Israel....

While the following are generalizations, they are generally true:

> Arabic-speaking people live in terrible, [closed] societies marked by massive injustice and poor prospects for improvement. Their lives are increasingly governed by restrictions based on religious interpretation, large-scale segregation by gender, a contrast of which they are well aware between the repression and stagnation of their own countries and the relative freedom and progress in other parts of the world...

There is deep resentment of the West for past imperialism, its relative power and wealth and cultural and religious differences.

All of these factors are systematically fed to the masses on a daily basis by mosques, schools, leaders, opposition politicians, media and just about every other Arabic institution.

And yet we are to believe that this problem is entirely or almost entirely caused by Israel's existence, the Arab-Israeli conflict and the situation of the Palestinians. That's it? Why do people say this? One reason is ignorance. The conflict is all they know about the Middle East, and this answer is what they are constantly told by most experts and some media. Another reason is politics, as it is a talking point by those who for various reasons want to wipe Israel off the map or weaken it.[31]

Teachings from the Koran and from Sharia law deny the Jews any right to live on an earth that Muslims believe belongs to Allah, period. Christians, Buddhists, Taoists, and others have far fewer rights, if any, than Muslims. Fanatical organizations such as al Qaeda, Hamas, Hezbollah, Fatah, the PLO, Islamic State and all the jihadists, mullahs, ayatollahs and imams who support them believe it is the sacred duty of every Muslim to attempt to convert the infidels. If rejected, then all non-Muslims must be eradicated to purify planet Earth.

Unfortunately, few heed the words Jesus spoke concerning the House of Israel:

> For I was an hungered, and ye gave me no meat: I was thirsty, and ye gave me no drink: I was a stranger, and ye took me not in: naked, and ye clothed me not: sick, and in prison, and ye visited me not. Then shall they also answer him, saying, Lord, when saw we thee an hungered, or athirst, or a stranger, or naked, or sick, or in prison, and did not minister unto thee? Then shall he answer them, saying, Verily I say unto you, **Inasmuch as ye did it not to one of the least of these, ye did it not to me.** (Emphasis mine, Matthew 25:42-45, KJV)

In the above verses, our Lord was referring to the Jews, His earthly seed. This Scripture means just what it says, and the United States finds itself at a critical crossroad: Do we believe the God of the Bible and stand with Israel? Or will we turn our backs on the Jewish people and embrace the Liberal Left views of those who commiserate with Israel's enemies? Many Americans embrace the *thought* of religion, but have turned their backs on its *reality*—an adherence to the Word of God.

Since 9/11 the U.S. has been embroiled in a war against radical Islamic groups. Our homeland has been made more vulnerable by the refusal to call a terrorist a terrorist. Those who desire to see the demise of the United States are often referred to erroneously as "freedom fighters." Presidents over the past few decades have pressed Israel not to retaliate against those fanatics who "only" want to see the Jewish people annihilated. Israel has further been compelled to give up land for peace—a futile exercise. In the entire chapter of Joel 3:1-17, God calls the nations to account for their treatment of His people:

> In those days and at that time, when I restore the fortunes of Judah and Jerusalem, I will gather all nations and bring them down to the Valley of Jehoshaphat. There I will put them on trial for what they did to my inheritance, my people Israel, because they scattered my

people among the nations and **divided up my land.** (Emphasis mine, Joel 3:1-3, NIV)

The truth is that the Jews were totally rejected during the Holocaust, and that was the response by the average Christian to their cries. May it not be our retort today.

Some Americans may not be the only ones who feel the Jews are responsible; that same feeling is palpable among young Israeli pundits. Many of them feel that "Israel is a deeply flawed democracy twisted by special laws favoring Conservative religious Jews and Judaism, by racism and segregation, by the Law of Return, by a labyrinthine separatist wall, by an ethnocentric national anthem and a Davidic flag, and by other grievous offenses to Palestinian Arabs."[32]

Conversely, Christian Zionists acknowledge that an enormous debt of gratitude is owed to the Jews. They also understand what so many fail to recognize: The Jewish people are not the reason fanatical Muslims hate the United States. Rather, the Jews are allies in the continuing fight against world domination by Islam. Until September 11, 2001, the Israelis stood their ground alone against this threat, and still today are the first to be attacked by terrorists. Even though the Israeli Defense Forces do not fight shoulder to shoulder with American troops, the two military forces guard, preserve, and protect identical values.

Truthfully, all the world's nations may turn their collective backs on the Jews, but God will never forsake His people:

> For Israel hath not been forsaken, nor Judah
> of his God, of the LORD of hosts, though their
> land was filled with sin against the Holy One
> of Israel. (Jeremiah 51:5, KJV)

Some say the promises of God to the Jews have been revoked; that they now belong solely to the Church. If this were true, why didn't the Apostle Paul know it? If all the promises were revoked, why didn't John the Revelator know it? And why didn't our Lord and Savior who gave this revelation to John know it? You cannot read the book of Revelation without being aware of Israel from chapters seven through twenty-one. Israel is, and will always be, God's Miracle Nation.

Some use defiance as an occasion to deny their responsibility, saying the Jews are blind. But the Word contradicts that claim:

> For I tell you, you [Believers] will not see me
> again until you say, "Blessed is he who comes
> in the name of the Lord." (Matthew 23:39, NIV)

You cannot say you have been a blessing until you have done something to bless someone. While many professing Christians stood mute as six million Jews were murdered in our lifetime, how can we who have turned our backs on their pain expect the Jewish people to listen to anything we might have to say?

Intimidated Christians in Europe maintained their silence while Hitler's death camps spewed smoke and ashes across the landscape. If you were Jewish, how would you feel when Christians sing in their churches about Jews in the Bible (Moses, David, Jesus), yet do nothing to reach out in love to living Jews? What about when Christians remained silent as America forced Israel to give the world's most infamous terrorist organization, the PLO and its leaders, part of the Holy Land from which 10,000 terrorist attacks would be committed against innocent Jews?

Once the horrors of German concentration camps became a reality, Christian attitudes were transformed. People began to understand that the Jews had suffered horribly at the hands of the Nazis, and that their living conditions following the end of the war were equally as deplorable. A place of sanctuary was needed for those who had been so horribly abused; change was an absolute necessity. Perhaps a stimulus for any change was the understanding that if Palestine, the ancient homeland of the Jews, was not opened to Jewish immigration, those survivors would be cast on the mercy of other Western nations.

Once that decision was made, it was not long before groups such as the National Council of Churches (NCC), now a member of the World Council of Churches (WCC) founded in 1948, in conjunction with other organizations, began to denigrate the plan for a Jewish homeland in Israel. For decades, the WCC has pointedly castigated the Jews.

Paul C. Merkley, Professor Emeritus of History at Carleton University, Ottawa, Canada, wrote of the WCC:

> During the weeks previous to the Six-Day War of June 1967, when Nasser, the dictator of Egypt, was rallying the Arab world for a war of liquidation against Israel, the WCC remained silent. But immediately after Israel's victory, the WCC . . .

announced that it "cannot condone by silence territorial expansion by armed force."[33]

From that day forward, the WCC and its constituent denominational organizations have generally portrayed Israel's behavior to be in lockstep with Arab rhetoric. They believe and declare that all subsequent wars have been fomented by Israel for the purpose of further territorial gain and for the opportunity to incorporate innocent and abject Arab populations. (Ironically, those Arab men, women, and children would benefit far more greatly by being under Israeli administration.) The WCC pressed constantly through the 1970s and 1980s for America's official contact with the PLO and denounced Israel's punitive responses to terrorism and civil disruption. It denounced the Camp David Accords of 1978 for allegedly ignoring the national ambitions of the "Palestinians." Its consistent line is that "Israel's repeated defiance of international law, its continuing occupation and the impunity it has so long enjoyed are the fundamental causes of the present violence and threaten peace and security of both peoples."[34]

In September 2001, WCC representatives attending the UN Conference on Racism, Racial Discrimination,

Xenophobia, and Related Intolerance at Durban, South Africa, infamously led the demand to officially denounce Israel for "systematic perpetration of racist crimes including war crimes, acts of genocide, and ethnic cleansing."[35]

When organizations professing to be comprised of people who believe the Bible to be the Word of God turn their backs on His Chosen People, how can its members ever hope to enjoy the blessings promised to those who stand with Israel? The answer again lies in Genesis 12:3, where God promised Abraham that He would curse the individual who cursed Israel. Satan, the Enemy, knows that blessing Israel brings liberty and provision; while cursing the Jewish nation brings captivity and poverty. The writer of Proverbs offered this warning, "Then poverty will pounce on you like a bandit; scarcity will attack you like an armed robber." (Proverbs 6:11, NLT)

The Enemy would tempt you to turn your back on those God has called "blessed." Instead of succumbing to his wiles, take a stand and shout, "Satan, you can't have Israel! She belongs to God."

SCRIPTURE PRAYER FOR ISRAEL:

ISAIAH 45:3 ....Father, You are the God of Israel, and they are Your people.

ISAIAH 45:4 ....You named them, though they did not know You.

JEREMIAH 33:8,,,,,,,,Lord, cleanse them from their iniquities, and pardon all of their sins.

ISAIAH 45:17 ....Save them with an everlasting salvation.

ISAIAH 45:13 ....Raise them up in righteousness, and direct all their ways.

PSALM 25:22 ....Redeem Israel out of all of their troubles.

JOEL 3:16 ....Be a shelter for Your people,

JOEL 3:16 ....and the strength of the children of Israel.

JEREMIAH 33:9 ....Bring health and healing to them and to their land,

JEREMIAH 33:6 ....Revealing to them Your abundance of peace and truth.

EPHESIANS 1:18 ......Let the eyes of their understanding be enlightened.

EPHESIANS 1:17 ......Give them the spirit of wisdom and revelation

EPHESIANS 1:17 ......in the knowledge of our Lord Jesus Christ.

JEREMIAH 33:9 ....Let Israel be to You a name of praise,

JEREMIAH 33:9 ....and an honor before all the nations of the earth.

JEREMIAH 33:9 ....Proclaiming all the good You do for them,

JEREMIAH 33:9 ....and causing fear and trembling among the nations,

JEREMIAH 33:9 ....because of all the goodness and prosperity You provide for it.

JOEL 2:25 ....Restore everything that has been removed from them.

JOEL 2:19 ....Send them grain and new wine and oil to satisfy them.

PROVERBS 16:7 ....Make their enemies to be at peace with them

JOEL 2:19 ....and no longer let them be a reproach among the nations.

EZEKIEL 34:12.........Seek out Your sheep and deliver them

EZEKIEL 34:13.........from the peoples and countries where they were scattered,

EZEKIEL 34:13.........and bring them to their own land.

PSALM 122:6...........I pray for the peace of Jerusalem,

PSALM 122:6...........may they prosper that love you.

EZEKIEL 34:25.........Lord, cause their enemies to cease from the land.

EZEKIEL 34:26.........Make them and the places all around Jerusalem a blessing,

EZEKIEL 34:26.........and cause showers of blessings to come down in their season.

EZEKIEL 34:27.........Let Your people dwell safely in their land,

JEREMIAH 34:17 ......delivered from trouble from all the kingdoms of the earth.[36]

9

SILENCE IMPLIES CONSENT

For Zion's sake I will not keep silent, and for
Jerusalem's sake I will not be quiet,
until her righteousness goes forth as brightness,
and her salvation as a burning torch.

ISAIAH 62:1, NIV

WHEN IT BECAME blatantly apparent in the 1960s that many in Christian churches were turning a blind eye to the plight of the Israelis, Dr. Franklin H. Littell, chairman of the Department of Religion at Temple University, felt the call to confront the Church regarding its lack of response to the Nazi-led methodical murder of six million Jews. Dr. Littell was convinced that *"Qui tacet consentit"* (silence implies consent). The good doctor was appalled when much of the Church again remained silent in the weeks leading to the Six-Day War. He felt that the lack of response indicated compliance. Dr. Littell wrote that such passivity signaled acquiescence to the Arab mandate that Israel be driven into the sea.

As Israel worked to push back her enemies, Littell worked to resurrect among Protestant churches the spirit of support for the Jewish nation that had been evident in the ACPC. Following Israel's success on the battlefield, he introduced his new organization, Christians Concerned for Israel (CCI). It was, for Dr. Littell, a testament to the effectiveness of the other pro-Israel organizations that had come before.

In 1978, the CCI became the embryo for the National Christian Leadership Conference of Israel, a much larger group whose foundation was laid during the congressional hearings to authorize the sale of AWACS (Airborne Warning and Control System) to Saudi Arabia. The sale was contested by Prime Minister Begin, as well as Senators Edward Kennedy and Bob Packwood. Despite the opposition, the sale of AWACS was finally approved by Congress in October 1981. Christians representing organizations across the United States amassed in Washington, D.C., to protest the sale. Many of the organizers were amazed at the number who responded to show their support for Israel and the determination and emotion that was exhibited.

Even though ridiculed, reviled, and rebuffed by many of the mainline churches, Christian Zionists have continued to support Israel. These dedicated men and women continue to battle anti-Semitism through both the written and spoken word. The support of Evangelicals for the descendants of Abraham, Isaac, and Jacob is genuine and should not be dismissed as irrelevant.

In light of all the biblical evidence presented until now, we must conclude that Christians have a God-given mandate to honor the Jewish people, wherever they are. But how does this connect to modern Israel? Many Christians seem happy enough to embrace Jewish neighbors living alongside them in largely Gentile lands, but are indifferent or even hostile to the proposition that we also have a duty to support the controversial State of Israel. Some Believers bristle at the mere suggestion that God has anything to do with Israel's amazing restoration in our era.

Centuries before the Jewish people first were forced into foreign captivity, God revealed that they would be expelled from their covenant land due to sin. But He also promised to eventually restore them to the Promised Land. This prophecy came via Moses—whose parents came from the tribe of Levi—while he was in the process of boldly leading the children of Israel from the bondage of Egypt into Canaan:

> That the Lord your God will bring you back from captivity, and have compassion on you, and gather you again from all the nations where the Lord your God has scattered you. (Deuteronomy 30:3, NKJV)

This prophecy could only be addressing the return of the Jewish people from Assyrian and Babylonian captivity hundreds of years before the time of Christ. Yet the ancient Hebrew prophets also foretold that Israel's loving God would restore His people to their Promised Land in the Last Days of history, just before Messiah begins His reign in Jerusalem. This implies that the Jews would be exiled two times from their beloved homeland, which is exactly what has historically taken place.

The prophets also foretold that the final Jewish ingathering would be from all over the globe, unlike the first return from lands directly to the east of Israel. It would be a permanent return, meaning no additional exiles would follow. Most significantly, it would end with the spiritual revival that King Solomon prophesied in 2 Chronicles 7:14:

> If My people who are called by My name will
> humble themselves, and pray and seek My face,
> and turn from their wicked ways, then I will
> hear from heaven, and will forgive their sin
> and heal their land. (II Chronicles 7:14, NKJV)

There are many prophetic Scriptures about this important topic in the Bible—far too many to quote them all here. But let's take a look at three of them:

> I will bring back the captives of My people
> Israel; They shall build the waste cities and
> inhabit them; They shall plant vineyards and
> drink wine from them; They shall also make
> gardens and eat fruit from them. I will plant
> them in their land, And no longer shall they
> be pulled up From the land I have given them,'
> Says the Lord your God. (Amos 9:14-15, NKJV)

> "For behold, the days are coming," says the
> Lord, "'that I will bring back from captivity My
> people Israel and Judah," says the Lord. "And
> I will cause them to return to the land that I
> gave to their fathers, and they shall possess it."
> (Jeremiah 30:3, NKJV)

Who hath heard such a thing? who hath seen such things? Shall the earth be made to bring forth in one day? or shall a nation be born at once? for as soon as Zion travailed, she brought forth her children. Shall I bring to the birth , and not cause to bring forth? saith the LORD: shall I cause to bring forth , and shut the womb? saith thy God. Rejoice ye with Jerusalem, and be glad with her, all ye that love her: rejoice for joy with her, all ye that mourn for her: That ye may suck, and be satisfied with the breasts of her consolations; that ye may milk out, and be delighted with the abundance of her glory. For thus saith the LORD, Behold, I will extend peace to her like a river, and the glory of the Gentiles like a flowing stream: then shall ye suck, ye shall be borne upon her sides, and be dandled upon her knees. As one whom his mother comforteth, so will I comfort you; and ye shall be comforted in Jerusalem. (Isaiah 66:8-13, KJV)

As mentioned previously, the Hebrew prophets also revealed that the full ingathering of the scattered Jewish people would only be completed when the Messiah came to earth. In other words, some Jews will still be living outside of Israel during the end of this age. However, this does not lessen or negate the fact that a large-scale return has been occurring in our day. In fact, nearly half the Jews on Earth have now returned to their biblical Promised Land. Christians worldwide should be exuberant supporters of this prophesied restoration, for it confirms that the God of Israel exists, that the prophecies of the Bible are true. God holds the future in His capable hands. He is a covenant-keeping Lord, and a merciful God who forgives the sins of His people.

Sometimes Christians ask me, "How do I know if my church is a Bible-believing church that doesn't teach replacement theology, progressive dispensationalism, or supersessionism?"

Ask yourself these questions:

- ❖ Does my pastor encourage the church to pray for the Jewish people, for the peace of Jerusalem and Israel?

- ❖ Does my pastor teach on Israel and its biblical significance?

- ❖ Does my pastor teach on the significance of the Church's Jewish roots?

✧ Does my pastor teach against the doctrines of replacement theology or supersessionism?

If the answer to these questions is "No," then you may be a member of a church that refuses to believe the Bible, and rejects God's eternal promises to the House of Israel. If your church seems powerless, and appears not to be blessed by God, perhaps this is the reason.

We must be part of God's dream team and support Israel and the Jewish people. Their existence and the rebirth of Israel is a miracle. As Christians, we believe in miracles; the resurrection of our Lord was the greatest of all miracles. If He can live again, it is no problem at all for Him to restore the Nation of Israel.

Israel was not born in 1948; she was born in the heart of God and revealed to Abraham many years before the birth of Isaac. God made a blood covenant with Abraham that the land of Canaan would be given to his seed through Isaac (Genesis 15:18). As part of the vision, God revealed to Abraham that for 400 years his seed would be strangers in a land which did not belong to them (Genesis 15:13). The offspring of Isaac spent 400 years in Egypt before

Moses miraculously led them out, and Israel, the nation, was born.

Unique as this religious centrality is, there is one reason above all others why committed Christians must stand with Israel: The God of the Universe, the God that we worship, has chosen to make an *everlasting* covenant with the physical descendants of Abraham, Isaac, and Jacob—the Jewish people.

The word "everlasting" has nothing temporary or conditional about it. It clearly means, "Lasting forever." Although Jews in number are found today in North and South America, Australia, Asia, Europe, many parts of Africa, and virtually every non-Muslim nation on earth, their historic spiritual and physical center has always been the Promised Land of Israel.

God's eternal covenant with the descendants of Abraham featured the promise to give them the land of Israel as an everlasting possession. This is recorded in the very first book of the Bible, Genesis, in chapter 17:

> When Abram was ninety-nine years old, the Lord appeared to Abram and said to him, "I am Almighty God; walk before Me and be blameless.

And I will make My covenant between Me and you, and will multiply you exceedingly." Then Abram fell on his face, and God talked with him, saying: "As for Me, behold, My covenant is with you, and you shall be a father of many nations. No longer shall your name be called Abram, but your name shall be Abraham; for I have made you a father of many nations. I will make you exceedingly fruitful; and I will make nations of you, and kings shall come from you. And I will establish My covenant between Me and you and your descendants after you in their generations, for an everlasting covenant, to be God to you and your descendants after you. Also I give to you and your descendants after you the land in which you are a stranger, all the land of Canaan, as an everlasting possession; and I will be their God." (Genesis 17:1-8, NKJV)

It is true God reveals in these verses that many peoples will eventually emerge from Abraham's loins, and so it has been. The Arabs, scattered in over 20 countries throughout the Middle East and North Africa, trace their ancestry to the ancient patriarch who traveled to Canaan at God's command from the town of Ur in Chaldea. Their lineage comes through Abraham's first-born son, Ishmael. However, the Scriptures go on to reveal that the special, eternal land covenant, and others, will come through the line of the son of promise, Isaac, his grandson, Jacob, and his twelve great-grandsons—the forefathers of the modern Jewish people. This is summarized in Psalm 105, verses 8 through 11, NKJV:

> He remembers His covenant forever, The word which He commanded, for a thousand generations, The covenant which He made with Abraham, And His oath to Isaac, And confirmed it to Jacob for a statute, To Israel as an everlasting covenant, Saying, 'To you I will give the land of Canaan As the allotment of your inheritance.

As we have seen, the belief that God has revoked His solemn land covenant with the Jewish people due to their sin and rebellion against Him is widespread in the Church today. It is certainly a fact that living peacefully in the land was conditional on obedience to God's holy law. Jacob's offspring were warned that they would be removed from the land if they disobeyed God's commands.

But the Bible also foretells that a Jewish remnant would be restored to the Promised Land after worldwide exile, as is wonderfully occurring in our day.

The proclamation "next year in Jerusalem" became a part of the Passover Seder during the Middle Ages. It was an expression of the longing of the Jewish people that Jerusalem and the Temple be rebuilt. Today Jerusalem stands, reunified under Jewish rule. It is a flourishing and modern city to which Jews of the Diaspora, forced from home and land through the centuries, have returned. In Psalm 137, the Jews carried away to Babylon sat down and wept as they remembered their homeland and the Holy City:

> There on the poplars we hung our harps, for there our captors asked us for songs, our tor-mentors demanded songs of joy; they said, "Sing us one of the songs of Zion!" How can we sing the songs of the LORD while in a foreign land? If I forget you, Jerusalem, may my right hand forget its skill. May my tongue cling to the roof of my mouth if I do not remember you, if I do not consider Jerusalem my highest joy. (Psalm 137:2-6, NIV)

The captives did not dash their harps against the rocks around them; their musical instruments were hung on trees that dotted the landscape, preserved for a future time—in the Holy City. It was symbolic of the hope of their return to Jerusalem when sorrow would be turned into joy, mourning into dancing, their ashes exchanged for beauty, and the spirit of heaviness replaced with the garment of praise (see Isaiah 61:3.)

Jehovah God preserved a remnant of His people down through the ages despite Satan's attempts to totally annihilate the Israelites. Jehovah-Mephalti, the Lord my Deliverer, declared: "And you who are left in Judah, who have escaped the ravages of the siege, will put roots down in your own soil and grow up and flourish." (Isaiah 37:31, NLT) Despite Satan's tactics, he cannot halt God's blessings on His Chosen People.

PRAYER FOR ISRAEL:
(FOR DELIVERANCE FROM THE ENEMY)

Contend, LORD, with those who contend with me; fight against those who fight against me. Take up shield and armor; arise and come to my aid. Brandish spear and javelin against those who pursue me. Say to me, "I am your salvation." May those who seek my life be disgraced and put to shame; may those who plot my ruin be turned back in dismay. Do not let those gloat over me who are my enemies without cause; do not let those who hate me without reason maliciously wink the eye. They do not speak peaceably, but devise false accusations against those who live quietly in the land. May those who delight in my vindication shout for joy and gladness; may they always say, "The LORD be exalted, who delights in the well-being of his servant. (Psalm 35:1-4, 19-20, 27)

SCRIPTURES FOR STUDY:

Psalm 35	Romans 11:18-20
Romans 11:2	Romans 11:1-2
Romans 9:4-5	James 1:1
Ezekiel 28:25-26	Isaiah 11:12
Ezekiel 36:24	Jeremiah 33:7-8

10

GOD ALMIGHTY HAS PRESERVED ISRAEL

Behold, He who keeps Israel Shall neither slumber nor sleep. The Lord is your keeper; The Lord is your shade at your right hand. The sun shall not strike you by day, Nor the moon by night. The Lord shall preserve you from all evil; He shall preserve your soul. The Lord shall preserve your going out and your coming in From this time forth, and even forevermore."

PSALM 121:4-8, KJV

GOD HAS NOT PERMITTED any power to totally exterminate the Jews, although no people have been plagued, persecuted, pursued, and pressured more throughout their history. Many attempts at annihilation have been made, but all have ended in utter failure, defeat, and humiliation.

Author George Gilder wrote:

In *Dialogues and Secrets with Kings*, published after the 1967 war, the very first official... PLO leader, Ahmad Shuqeiri [said], "I frequently called upon Arabs to liquidate the state of Israel and to throw the Jews into the sea. I said this because I was—and still am—convinced that there is no solution other than the elimination of the state of Israel."[37]

Take a step back in time and look at Egypt and Pharaoh's edict concerning the Israelites:

So Pharaoh commanded all his people, saying, "Every son who is born you shall cast into the river, and every daughter you shall save alive." (Exodus 1:22, NKJV)

Following Pharaoh's brutal treatment of the Children of Israel, God sent Moses to deliver His people from their harsh existence under the Egyptian ruler. In order to change the heart of the Pharaoh, God sent a series of ten plagues against the captors. The first three curses affected the comfort of the Egyptian people. By turning the water to blood, He denied them what was needed for cleansing and drinking. The Nile River, also worshipped as the giver of life, became instead an agent of death. Secondly, their homes were invaded by frogs. (I have never been able to understand why, as Moses asked Pharaoh when he would like to be rid of the frogs, he said, "Tomorrow." Why did he want to spend another night with the slimy, green amphibians?) Thirdly, lice invaded the land, attacking the Egyptians.

When Pharaoh continued to refuse to let God's people go, a second trifecta of plagues was unleashed on the land. They targeted Egypt's false gods. The fourth plague was that of flies, perhaps to let it be known that one of their gods, Beelzebub, lord of the flies, was incapable of rescuing them from Jehovah's wrath. The fifth plague decimated their herds of cattle. Again Jehovah proved He was greater than Apis, the sacred bull worshipped by the Egyptians. And the sixth challenged the claims of Egyptian medical shamans by causing a horrific outbreak of incurable boils. Still, Pharaoh was not moved to release the people to Moses, God's chosen leader.

The last set of three plagues was designed to bring death and desolation as hail rained down on the land flattening crops and killing more cattle. That was followed by a plague of locusts that stripped any green vegetation remaining after the hailstorms. Then darkness descended upon the land—so comprehensive that the Bible says:

> During all that time the people could not see each other, and no one moved. But there was light as usual where the people of Israel lived. (Exodus 10:23, NLT)

In Carlsbad Caverns, New Mexico, at one point during the tour, the guide asks everyone to sit. The lights are then turned off in the huge room for a few moments; the darkness is complete. You literally cannot see your hand held in front of your face. Imagine: God caused just such a blackness to cover the land of Egypt for three long days. Not a chariot moved; not a shaman prognosticated; no fishermen fished, and no merchant plied his trade.

With a still obstinate Pharaoh refusing to heed the warnings of Moses, God brought forth the tenth and final plague: the death of all the firstborn in Egypt—at least among those not safe beneath the blood covering of the Passover lamb.

Theologian Arthur W. Pink wrote of the tenth plague:

> One more judgment was appointed, the heaviest of them all, and then not only would Pharaoh

let the people go, but he would thrust them out.
Then would be clearly shown the folly of fighting
against God. Then would be fully demonstrated
the uselessness of resisting Jehovah. Then would
be made manifest the impotence of the creature
and the omnipotence of the Most High.[38]

Moses was vitally aware of what was about to befall
the Egyptian people. As a baby, he was saved by Pharaoh's
daughter because of an edict that demanded the deaths of
all male babies born to the children of Israel. The king's
disobedience would exact a dire penalty, not only upon
his household but also upon each individual in the land of
Egypt. Harsh, yes, but Pharaoh had been given numerous
opportunities to heed the voice of Jehovah. Because He is
a God of love, a way was made for the Israelites to escape
the sentence of death that had been pronounced, but the
Egyptians chose instead to ignore the warnings—all ten
of them in the form of the various plagues visited upon
the land.

The ruler who had so persecuted the children of
Abraham, Isaac, and Jacob, who had ordered every Hebrew
male child tossed into the Nile River lost every eldest son
in the land. For some families, it might have meant the

death of every male in the household—grandfather, father, eldest son, grandson. But Jehovah God didn't stop there: while pursuing the Hebrew children into the wilderness the entire Egyptian army was drowned in the Red Sea as Pharaoh watched helplessly. God had inexorably triumphed over the enemy of His children:

> Then Moses and the children of Israel sang this song to the LORD, and spoke, saying: "I will sing to the LORD, For He has triumphed gloriously! The horse and its rider He has thrown into the sea!" (Exodus 15:1, NKJV)

The Old Testament book of Esther paints a beautiful picture of God's deliverance of the Jews from the menace of anti-Semitism. Esther, a beautiful young Jewish girl, was torn from her home and taken captive to the palace. There, a tyrannical ruler had banished his queen from the royal throne and initiated a search for her successor. The king was captivated by Esther and chose her to be his new queen. As in any high drama, there was also a dastardly villain, Haman, who desired to perpetrate genocide against her Jewish people.

> Then Haman said to King Ahasuerus, "There is

> a certain people scattered and dispersed among
> the people in all the provinces of your kingdom;
> their laws are different from all other people's,
> and they do not keep the king's laws. Therefore
> it is not fitting for the king to let them remain."
> (Esther 3:8, NIV)

Esther's uncle, Mordecai, challenged Esther to approach the king (a move that could be punishable by death) and ask for the salvation of her people. In encouraging her to do so, Mordecai confronted Esther with these timeless words:

> For if you remain completely silent at this time,
> relief and deliverance will arise for the Jews
> from another place, but you and your father's
> house will perish. Yet who knows whether you
> have come to the kingdom for such a time as
> this? (Esther 4:14, NIV)

Esther's response to Mordecai was magnificent in its faith:

> Go, gather all the Jews who are present in
> Shushan, and fast for me; neither eat nor drink
> for three days, night or day. My maids and I

will fast likewise. And so I will go to the king, which is against the law; and if I perish, I perish! (Esther 4:16, NIV)

With great trepidation, Esther approached King Ahasuerus. Miraculously, he granted her an audience. The plan for the destruction of the Jews by the foul villain, Haman, was thwarted, and the king issued a decree throughout the land allowing Esther's people to defend themselves if attacked. Because of this decree, the Jews overcame every enemy and lived in peace (see Esther 8-9). Yet another attempt by Satan to annihilate the Jews was foiled.

Another major example was Satan's endeavor to destroy the Jews during World War II. Germany's leader, Adolf Hitler, declared the Jews were not the Chosen People, that the Aryan race was. He determined to resolve what he called the "Jewish problem," and disseminated the belief that the Jewish people were responsible for anarchy, dishonesty, and the ruin of civilization, government, and finance. According to those so-called "learned men," the purpose of the Jew was to completely weaken Germany and dilute the superior Aryan race.

The mustachioed little man mesmerized his listeners with a gravelly, impassioned voice — never mind that his speeches contained little of actual value. Near the end of 1921, he had come to be known as the *der Führer* (The Leader). History reveals that Adolf Hitler and his "Final Solution" was responsible for the deaths of six million Jewish men, women and children while the world turned a blind eye to his determination to destroy. This "hide your head in the sand" attitude allowed Hitler, the Nazi Party and its minions to fabricate a massive falsehood against the Jewish people.

The preservation of a remnant of Jews through all the suffering, wars and afflictions over the centuries is further evidence that Israel and the Jewish people are God's miracle. Why have the Jews been hated so? Because Satan's only adversary would come through the Jews: The Messiah. Ultimately He would destroy the powers of Satan.

Our God keeps His covenants; He remains faithful even when we are faithless (see 2 Timothy 2:13). It is He who has sovereignly decided to preserve the Jewish people as a separate, identifiable people before Him and then to restore them to their biblical homeland. These truths are revealed in numerous Scriptures. That they would remain on Earth until the end of time as a distinct people group is foretold in Jeremiah, Chapter 31:

> Thus says the Lord, Who gives the sun for a light by day, The ordinances of the moon and the stars for a light by night, Who disturbs the sea, And its waves roar (The Lord of hosts is His name): "If those ordinances depart From before Me, says the Lord, Then the seed of Israel shall also cease From being a nation before Me forever. (Jeremiah 31:35-36, NKJV)

The next verse makes it crystal clear that the God of Abraham has no intention of ever forsaking His special covenant with Jacob's children, despite their many failures:

> I will direct their work in truth, And will make with them an everlasting covenant. Their descendants shall be known among the Gentiles, And their offspring among the people. All who see them shall acknowledge them, That they are the posterity whom the Lord has blessed. (Isaiah 61:8-9, NKJV)

God calls the land of Israel, "My Land" (Ezekiel 38:16), and He gave it to Israel through a blood covenant that cannot be annulled. God has assigned the land of Israel to the children of Israel, and has never cancelled that which He assigned.

God said that Israel would be scattered among the heathen, and they were. The Enemy must have thought surely that his plan was working. But God also said they would be re-gathered, and they have been. As Believers, it is up to you and me to take up the banner of Jehovah-Gador Milchamah, the Lord Mighty in Battle and say to the Enemy, "Satan, you can't have Israel!"

PRAYER FOR ISRAEL:

Precious Father,

I come before Your throne and I bind every principality and power that is trying to destroy Your precious people, Israel. I love the Jewish people. Father, I pray that every demonic spirit will be bound in the mighty name of the Lord, and that You would pour out a river of healing upon the land of Israel and upon Your people. David said in Psalm 20:7, "Some trust in chariots and some in horses, but we trust in the name of the Lord our God," to help us defeat the Enemy.

SCRIPTURES FOR STUDY:

Psalm 24:8	Isaiah 11:12
Amos 9:14	Ezekiel 36:24
Jeremiah 32:37	Amos 9:15
Isaiah 43:6	Isaiah 49:22
Isaiah 60:8-9	Amos 9:14-15

11

BLESSINGS ABUNDANTLY

*Happy are you, O Israel! Who is like you,
a people saved by the LORD, The shield of
your help And the sword of your majesty!
Your enemies shall submit to you, And you
shall tread down their high places."*

DEUTERONOMY 33:29, NKJV

JUST AS GOD BLESSES those who stand with Israel, so He has blessed His Chosen People. Media focus on this tiny Middle Eastern country is normally consumed with conflicts between the Jews and their neighbors who decry the very existence of God's Chosen People. Rather than be cowed by all the negative attention derived from international criticism, Israelis have chosen to take the high road and continue to produce inventions and discoveries, and boast a society that benefits the world population in general.

The culture of Israel combines some of the best of Eastern ethnic and religious traditions, along with those of Western civilization. The cities of Tel Aviv and Jerusalem are considered by most to be the artistic centers of the country.

Ethnicity is represented by immigrants from five continents and more than one hundred countries. Significant subcultures are added by the Arabs, Russian Jews, Ethiopian Jews and the Ultra-Orthodox. All the while, it is a family-oriented society with a strong sense of community.

In the nineteenth and twentieth centuries, the then-existing culture was infused with both the mores and traditions of those who had lived outside Palestine or modern Israel. David Ben-Gurion led the trend of blending the many immigrants who began arriving from Europe, North Africa, and Asia into one melting pot that would unify newer immigrants with veteran Israelis.

Gradually, Israeli society has become more interconnected. Critics consider it to have been a necessity in the first years of the reborn state, but now aver that there is no longer a need for it. Others, mainly Mizrahi Jews (descended from local communities of the Middle East, as opposed to those from Europe), along with Holocaust survivors, have criticized the earlier move to unify the country. According to them, they were forced to conceal their diaspora heritage and philosophies brought from other countries, and adopt a new Sabra culture. The word 'Sabra' originally described the new Jew that had emerged in Palestine, particularly when contrasted with the old Jew from overseas.

Since the Jewish infusion from other countries, classical music in Israel has been especially vibrant as hundreds of music teachers and students, composers, instrumentalists and singers, as well as thousands of music lovers, streamed into the country, driven initially by the threat of Nazism in Europe. Israel is home to several world-class classical music ensembles, such as the Israel Philharmonic and the New Israeli Opera. The founding of The Palestine Philharmonic Orchestra (today's Israel Philharmonic Orchestra) in 1936 marked the beginning of Israel's classical music scene. In the early 1980s, the New Israeli Opera began staging productions, reviving public enthusiasm for operatic works. Russian immigration in the 1990s boosted the classical music genre with new talents and music lovers.

The Israel Philharmonic Orchestra performs at venues throughout the country and abroad, and almost every city has its own orchestra, many of the musicians having emigrated from the former Soviet Union. Israeli filmmakers and thespians have won acclimation at international film festivals. In recent years, Jewish literature has been widely translated, and several Israeli writers have gained international recognition.

While Hebrew and Arabic are the official languages of the State, an incredible 83 tongues are spoken in the country. As new immigrants began to arrive, learning Hebrew became a national goal. Special schools for the teaching of Hebrew were set up all over the country.

The initial works of Hebrew literature in Israel were written by authors rooted in the world and traditions of European Jewry. Native-born writers who published their works in the 1940s and 1950s, often called the "War of Independence generation," brought the Sabra mentality and culture to their writing.

From the beginning of the twentieth century, visual arts in Israel have shown a creative orientation, influenced both by the West and East, as well as by the land itself. Their developments, the character of the cities, and stylistic trends have been imported from art centers abroad. In painting, sculpture, photography, and other art forms, the country's varied landscape is prominent: the hill terraces and ridges produce special dynamics of line and shape; the foothills of the Negev, the prevailing grayish-green vegetation, and the clear luminous light result in distinctive color effects; and the sea and sand affect surfaces. Local landscapes, concerns, and politics ensure the uniqueness of Israeli art.

Traditional folk music of Israel includes the Hora and Yemenite dances. Modern dance in Israel has won international acclaim. Israeli choreographers are considered to be among the most versatile and original international creators working today. Notable dance companies include the Batsheva Dance Company and the Kibbutz Contemporary Dance Company. People come from all over Israel and many other nations for the annual dance festival staged each July in Karmiel. It is the largest celebration of dance in Israel, featuring three or four days and nights of dancing, with 5,000 or more dancers and a quarter of a million spectators visiting the capital of Galilee. Begun as an Israeli folk dance event, festivities now include performances, workshops, and open dance sessions featuring a variety of dance forms and nationalities. Famous companies and choreographers from all over the world have come to Israel to perform and give master classes.

Israel has the highest number of museums per capita in the world, with over 200 bringing millions of visitors annually. Jerusalem's Israel Museum has a special pavilion showcasing the Dead Sea scrolls and a large collection of Jewish religious art, Israeli art, sculptures and Old Masters paintings. Yad Vashem, the nation of Israel's memorial to Holocaust victims, is one of the most visited and revered sites in the country. The holy halls preserve and cherish memories of those who perished in ovens fired by hatred, and disclose the lessons learned for future generations.

In September 2015, the Friends of Zion Heritage Center and Museum was officially opened and dedicated. It has long been a dream of mine to make it possible for the Jewish people and the world to know the love that millions have for God's Chosen People. What a milestone for my vision and the future of Israel to see its doors opened! Through this marvelous museum, we tell the stories of Heroes of the Faith who sacrificed everything—including some of whom sacrificed their very lives—to protect the Jewish People.

Israel's diverse culture is manifested in its cuisine, a combination of local ingredients and dishes and diasporic dishes from around the world. An Israeli 'fusion' cuisine has developed, with the adoption and continued adaptation of elements of various Jewish cuisine along with other foods traditionally eaten in the Middle East. Israeli cuisine is understandably influenced by geography, featuring foods common in the Mediterranean region such as olives, chickpeas, dairy products, fish, and fresh fruits and vegetables.

The main meal is usually lunch rather than dinner. Jewish holidays influence the cuisine, with many traditional foods served. Shabbat (the Jewish day of rest and seventh day of the week) dinner, eaten on Friday night, is a significant meal in many Israeli homes. While not all Jews in Israel keep kosher, the observance of *kashrut* influences the menu in numerous homes, public institutions and many restaurants. Kashrut is the set of Jewish dietary laws. Food that may be consumed according to Jewish law is termed "kosher" in English, or fit for consumption. Most of the basic laws of kashrut are derived from the Torah's Books of Leviticus and Deuteronomy. While the Torah does not state the rationale for most kashrut laws, many reasons have been suggested, including philosophical, practical and hygienic.

Since physical fitness is important in Jewish culture, the Maccabiah Games, an Olympic-style event for Jewish athletes, was inaugurated in the 1930s. The games have been held in Israel every four years since then.

At this writing, Israelis have won seven Olympic medals dating from their initial victories in 1992, including a gold medal in windsurfing at the 2004 Summer Olympics. Unquestionably the most memorable Olympics took place in 1972 in Munich, Germany, when members of Black September, a militant extremist group with ties to Arafat's Fatah organization, took eleven members of Israel's Olympic team hostage. After hours of negotiations between the leaders of the terrorist group and the German police, the eleven Israelis, five terrorists, and one German police officer would die during a bloody gun battle at the NATO airbase in Firstenfeldbruck.

Jealousy could likely be the reason fundamental Islamists fanatically target not only the Jews in Israel but the United States' citizens, according to noted Jewish lecturer, Irwin N. Graulich:

In addition, during that same period [1948–current], Israel totally embarrassed the entire Arab/Muslim world by defeating them economically, technologically, intellectually, culturally, religiously, medically, socially and morally. Since America's accomplishments are that much greater, it is no wonder that the Arab/Muslim nations feel totally frustrated. They subscribe to a religious belief that promises world greatness, strength and domination, while reality shows them trailing very far behind.[39]

Not only are there numerous inventive and creative people in Israel, there is a sense of generosity and compassion few of its neighbors deign to recognize and/or accept. For example, a *World News* article on NBC.com revealed a heartwarming story of unheralded assistance to a family in Syria:

The young girl was dying when she arrived in the land of her country's enemy. A heart condition had left the 4-year-old Syrian struggling to walk or even talk. But in Israel—a country still in a state of cease-fire with Syria after the Yom Kippur War four decades ago—she found her saviors. Admitted in early 2013 to the Wolfson Medical Center, south of Tel Aviv, she underwent life-saving surgery. The girl is now recuperating on a ward along with children from the West Bank and Gaza Strip, Sudan, Romania, China and Israel. "She would have definitely died if she wouldn't have arrived here," Ilan Cohen, one of the doctors who treated her, said. "A lot of patients arrive here from enemy countries and view Israelis as demons. They are surprised that we are human without horns on our heads," he added. "This is the first time they see Israelis without a uniform and I think it's a good surprise." Her treatment was the work of "Save a Child's Heart," an Israeli nonprofit organization started by the late Ami Cohen, who moved to Israel from the United States in 1992. He joined the staff of the Wolfson with a vision to mending children's hearts from around the world. The organization he began has since helped treat 3,200 children from 45 countries.[40]

The story told of the mother's fear of reprisal upon their return home. It seems incredible that hatred could be so strong as to fault a family for trying to save a beloved child; and yet it is. The other side of that story is the men and women who provided the techniques and services that saved the life of the young girl.

In the sixty-five-plus years since Israel was recognized as a state in the mid-1940s, amazing strides have been made in science, technology, medicine, farming, and communication thanks to the diligence of the people who live in the Holy Land.

There have been some mind-boggling discoveries in the field of medicine, to wit:

⋄ In 1954, Ephraim Frei discovered the effects of magnetism on the human body. His exploration led to the advancement of the T-scan system, a breakthrough in the advancement for detecting breast cancer.

⋄ In 1956, Professor Leo Sachs developed amniocentesis to uncover the benefits of examining amniotic fluid in the diagnosis of prenatal anomalies. It has become a major obstetrics tool in aiding pregnant women and their unborn babies. In 1963, Sachs became the first to grow lab-bred

blood cells, a tool used to help chemo-
therapy patients.

✧ Ada Yonath, awarded the Nobel Prize in
Chemistry in 2009, laid the groundwork
for the advent of drugs that are used to
treat some strains of leukemia, glaucoma
and HIV, as well as antipsychotic and anti-
depressant medicines.

✧ The time it takes to heal a broken bone
may soon be cut in half thanks to an
intelligent "wrapping paper" from Israeli
company Regenecure. The "wrapping
paper," technically called a membrane
implant, enables bones to heal faster and
more evenly by attracting healing stem
cells and fluids while keeping soft tissues
from growing around the broken bone.
The membrane looks and feels like plastic
wrap, it can be cut with a pair of scissors
to fit any bone in the body and is naturally
absorbed into the body after 10 months.
The material has already been used in
dental procedures to replace bone grafts

and has been used on animal bones, where
it cut the healing time in half when used
along with a traditional bone graft.[41]

Added to these inspired and ingenious men and women
are Meir Wilcheck, the discoverer of blood detoxification;
Elli Canaani, inventing a drug to treat chronic myelog-
enous leukemia; Avram Hershko and Aaron Ciechanover,
improving cellular research to better determine the cause
of ailments such as cervical cancer and cystic fibrosis;
and, the creation of Copaxone, the only non-interferon
treatment for multiple sclerosis. These are only a few of
the many advancements in detection and management of a
myriad of diseases and serious health conditions. Amazing
and innovative techniques have originated in the field of
spinal surgery, treatment of Parkinson's disease, tumor
and small bowel (Pillcam) imaging, in first-aid in the
form of innovative field dressings that are now the global
standard, the Lubocollar used to treat trauma patients
worldwide, helping paraplegics walk, treating diabetes,
artificial limb improvements, and more.

Israel has silently and steadily blossomed into an enthu-
siastic and impressive proving ground for entrepreneurs

and inventors. In the field of technology, just a few examples are:

- ✧ The Uzi machine gun developed by Major Uzi Gaf; millions are in use globally.

- ✧ The WEIZAC computer introduced by the Weizmann Institute in 1955 was one of the first, "large-scale stored program computers in the world."[42]

- ✧ A solar energy system that today is used to power the majority of hot water heaters worldwide. We must also include color holograms, desalination processes, drone aircraft, computer processors, digital information sharing, terrorist detectors, and thousands of other technology-based products.[43]

Farmers worldwide have enjoyed the benefits of advances such as the super cucumber and disease resistant potatoes, improved food storage systems, drip irrigation, extracting water from the air, bee preservation, advanced fish farming, water purification, and more ecologically-friendly food packaging.

Add to this list baby monitors, instant messaging, office equipment, the Babylon computer dictionary, flash drives, micro-computers, miniature video cameras, computer chips, advances in airport safety, and missile defense systems. It is an incredible list; a testament to the ingenuity and inventiveness of the Jewish people.

Many of these inventions have earned Nobel prizes for those responsible, but the awards are not confined to science and technology. Now, they are shared by authors, poets, mathematicians, peacemakers and economists.

It is amazing to discover that 22 percent of all individual Nobel Prize winners worldwide between the organization's inception in 1901 and 2015 have been of Jewish descent. That alone is an incredible number to contemplate.

Two Jewish laureates were honored after having endured incarceration in concentration camps during the Holocaust: Imre Kertész and Elie Wiesel. At the age of 14, Kertész was rounded up with other Hungarian Jews and sent first to Auschwitz, and then to Buchenwald. He is a prolific writer whose best-known novel, *Sorstalanság*, (Fatelessness) unveiled the experiences of a teenage boy who was sent to the camps at Auchwitz, Buchenwald, and Zeitz. He was awarded the Prize in 2002 "for writing that upholds the fragile experience of the individual against the barbaric arbitrariness of history."[44]

Elie Wiesel, who was also sent to Auschwitz, Buna, and Buchenwald during World War II, received the Nobel Prize in 1986. The committee characterized him as a "messenger to mankind," stating that through his struggle to come to terms with "his own personal experience of total humiliation and of the utter contempt for humanity shown in Hitler's death camps", as well as his "practical work in the cause of peace", Wiesel delivered a powerful message "of peace, atonement and human dignity" to humanity.[45]

It is incredibly overwhelming and unimaginable to consider how many life-changing inventions might have been lost at Auschwitz and Birkenau, only two of the many concentration camps where Jews were cruelly murdered during the Holocaust. Author Victoria J. Barnett wrote of the role of the Church during those dark and devastating years:

> European Jews [were] not a high priority of the Allied governments as they sought to defeat Hitler militarily. The courageous acts of individual rescuers and resistance members proved to be the exception, not the norm....this inertia

defined the organized Christian community as well. Churches throughout Europe were mostly silent while Jews were persecuted, deported and murdered. In Nazi Germany in September 1935, there were a few Christians in the Protestant Confessing Church who demanded that their Church take a public stand in defense of the Jews. Their efforts, however, were overruled by Church leaders who wanted to avoid any conflict with the Nazi regime. Internationally, some Church leaders in Europe and North America did condemn the Nazis' measures against the Jews, and there were many debates about how Christians outside Nazi Germany and Nazi-occupied territory should best respond to Hitler's brutal policies. These discussions, however, tended to become focused more on secondary strategic considerations—like maintaining good relations with colleagues in the German Churches—than on the central humanitarian issues that were really at stake. . . .

Reflecting on the failure of the Churches to challenge the Nazis should prompt us to ponder all the others—individuals, governments and institutions—that passively acquiesced to the

Third Reich's tyranny. Even the wisest and most perceptive of them, it seems, failed to develop adequate moral and political responses to Nazi genocide, failed to recognize that something new was demanded of them by the barbarism of Hitler's regime.[46]

In 2009, I was invited to speak at a communications and law conference held at Ariel University in Israel. It was my distinct privilege to meet Nobel Laureate, Professor Robert Aumann of Hebrew University, and founder of the Game Theory Society. I had been asked to attend the conference by my good friend, the late Ron Nachman, mayor of the city of Ariel, and was able to see firsthand the genius of the professor.

Born in Germany, Aumann and his family escaped just fourteen days before the ravages of *Kristallnacht*, a series of coordinated attacks against Jews in Nazi Germany and parts of Austria. In a 2005 Jerusalem Post article, journalist Hilary Leila Krieger wrote:

> The year was 1938 and the Aumanns desperately wanted to leave their native Germany. Salvation dangled in the form of US visas, available for

passport holders who swore they wouldn't be a burden on their new country and passed a test of basic American terms and concepts. Robert "Yisrael" Aumann saw his parents studying hard and thought he should do likewise. After his parents passed the exam, his mother confided in the consular official that her son had also prepared very diligently and would like to be presented with a test question. The consul leaned over to the eight-year-old and asked him to name the president of the United States— at the time Franklin D. Roosevelt. Aumann answered enthusiastically: "Rosenfeld!" The consul burst out laughing. He also granted the boy a visa. The qualities Aumann displayed at a ripe age—a propensity for hard work, a fierce intellect and a commitment to Jewish values—and has continued to exhibit throughout adulthood, earned him [the 2013] Nobel prize in economics.[47]

When presented with the Nobel Prize in 2005, the Professor titled his acceptance speech "War and Peace." He said to the assembled audience:

Simplistic peacemaking can cause war, while arms race, credible war threats and mutually assured destruction can reliably prevent war.[48]

Ernest Hemingway wrote: "The world breaks everyone, and afterward, some are strong at the broken places."[49] Adversity has forged a people of great strength, resiliency, insight, and intelligence. As the psalmist wrote in Psalm 115:12, ESV: "The LORD has remembered us; he will bless us; he will bless the house of Israel. . . "

The list of Nobel Prize-winning men and women who have sprung from Abraham, Isaac, and Jacob is long and impressive: Nelly Sachs, Shmuel Yosef Agnon, Saul Bellow, Ada Yonath, Isaac Bashevis Singer, Dan Shechtman, Menachem Begin, Yitzhak Rabin, and Shimon Peres.

However, brilliance, tenacity, and determination are not confined to Nobel Prize winners. It is found in all men and women whose goals are to work hard, teach their children, bless their neighbors, feed the hungry, extend a helping hand to those in need, and build on the foundations of the past to reap the blessings of Jehovah, He who blesses the House of Israel.

Twenty-first century Jewish scientists and inventors

can also be found at the forefront of invention and technological genius. Just as in past decades, Israelis are not simply marginal participants in new and innovative discoveries; they are at the very epicenter of modern ingenuity.

In recent years, however, the fight against Israel's very existence has taken yet another downward turn—targeting the nation's productivity. While Jewish men and women are working to make the world a better place, a demonic plan has been birthed in hell to destroy the nation of Israel—to literally bankrupt her and curse the nation. It is called BDS: Boycott, Divestment and Sanctions, and is all about economics. The plan is to turn worldwide public opinion against Israel, to isolate the Jewish nation, decimate her economy and reshape Israel into a pariah state which no one will be willing to defend.

Global pension funds have hastened to join this movement. The Rand Corporation reports that if this trend continues, the BDS movement will cost Israel more than $47 billion. Some of the most powerful names supporting BDS include George Soros, and even Bill Gates. Universities around the world are also behind the movement and count among their number some of America's leading schools.

According to the "BDS Victories" website, a number

of artists have joined the boycott against Israel including, "Bono, Snoop Dogg, Jean Luc Godard, Elvis Costello, Gil Scott Heron, Carlos Santana" and others.[50] And Israel is also being blacklisted. For example, both the Luxembourg Pension Fund and the Norway Pension Fund have nixed any involvement with Israel.

Perhaps the most heartbreaking thing about this demonic conspiracy is the number of church organizations that have been practicing divestment. The Presbyterian Church of the U.S.A. is part of this movement, as is the United Church of Christ, the United Methodist Church, the Quaker Friends Fiduciary Corporation and the Mennonite Central Committee. It is a narrative designed to curse Israel and break her economically. *Israel Today* reports:

> Last year, the Presbyterian Church (U.S.A.) voted to sell stock in a few companies whose products are used by Israel in the territories. The United Church of Christ resolution was broader. Delegates are calling on the denomination's financial arms to sell off stock in any company profiting from what the church called human rights violations arising from the occupation.

The church also voted to boycott Israeli products made in the territories.[51]

The Word of God is very explicit in the Genesis 12:3 admonition, "I [God] will bless them that bless thee"; and in the New Testament book of Luke:

> Give, and it will be given to you. A good measure, pressed down, shaken together and running over, will be poured into your lap. For with the measure you use, it will be measured to you. (Luke 6:38, NIV)

The Church of Jesus Christ today "needs to renew her understanding of her Jewish roots and reach out to the Jews with love and gratitude. . . If we turn our affections on the Jewish people we'll see more of God's blessings on the church."[52] This determination to stand with the Jewish people would bring revival to the Church. Then, united Believers would be able to "stand against the schemes of the devil" (see Ephesians 6:11, ESV) whose sole determination is to destroy the seed of Abraham.

PRAYER FOR ISRAEL:
(TO EQUIP THE SAINTS FOR SPIRITUAL WARFARE)

Father,

Israel and America need revival and restoration. Spiritual warfare is the method, Jesus is the key. He has provided me with weapons of warfare to pull down the strongholds of the Enemy. With the armor for protection, I have on truth, the breastplate of righteousness and on my feet I have the preparation of the Gospel of peace. I hold in one hand the shield of faith with which I can divert every fiery dart of the Enemy, and in the other I clutch the sword of the Spirit which is Your Word. You have said that no weapon formed against me shall prosper, and that the "weapons of our warfare are not carnal but mighty in God for pulling down strongholds, casting down arguments and every high thing that exalts itself against the knowledge of God." You have called me to "Submit to God. Resist the devil and he will flee from you." Therefore, I say to the Enemy, Satan, you can't have Israel and God's Chosen People, for greater is He that is in me than he that is in the world!

SCRIPTURES FOR STUDY:

II Corinthians 10:4-5   James 4:7   Ephesians 6:12

II Corinthians 10:3-4   Zechariah 4:6   John 16:33

Revelation 12:10   I Corinthians 16:13   Joshua 1:9

I Peter 5:8   Ephesians 6:18

12

THE VALUE OF INTERCESSORS

I have set watchmen upon thy walls, O Jerusalem,
which shall never hold their peace day nor night:
ye that make mention of the LORD, keep not
silence, And give him no rest, till he establish, and
till he make Jerusalem a praise in the earth.

ISAIAH 62:6-7, KJV

GOD HAS A PURPOSE and a plan for our lives. The lives of those in the United States as well as the nation of Israel are dependent on prayer. His will and His blessings are bound up in prayer. The fuel that moves the engine of humanity is prayer. Almighty God created the nation of Israel. His purposes and plans are more important than anything Man may accomplish. Conversely, to engage in prayer is one of the most crucial things we can do.

As Jeremiah prophesied to the Jewish people during their captivity in Babylon, he was given this promise by

God, "Call unto me, and I will answer thee, and shew thee great and mighty things, which thou knowest not." (Jeremiah 33:3, KJV) The Jews were ultimately delivered from captivity, and revival came to Israel.

Prayer is a vital part of our relationship with our Heavenly Father. If you were to ask any John Doe on the street to loan you $200, it is highly likely he would simply laugh. If, however, you were to approach someone of longstanding friendship—someone who knew that you were honest, honorable, and trustworthy, the odds of a loan being granted would increase exponentially. God wants His people to build a relationship with Him, to communicate with Him frequently, to trust Him and to recognize His sovereignty in our lives as did men such as Daniel, Abraham, and David. This is the only way to become equipped for spiritual warfare.

Abraham is a striking example of the power of prayer. For Lot's sake, he interceded for Sodom and God delayed judgment. He would have even spared Sodom for ten righteous souls (see Genesis 18:20-33). Abraham thought surely Lot, his wife, his daughters, his sons and sons-in-law would be righteous and total more than ten; he was wrong. Even Lot's wife paid the ultimate price when she turned to look longingly at the worldly treasures and pleasures she was leaving behind.

Wherever Abraham, a praying man, pitched his tent and camped for a season with his household, he erected an altar of sacrifice and of prayer. In another example, God said in a dream to Abimelech, king of Gerar, Abraham "is a prophet, and he shall pray for thee, and thou shalt live." (See Genesis 20:7, KJV)

God heard Abraham's prayers, and He hears ours. Moses interceded forty days for Israel. The result was a mighty deliverance for the nation. God's movement to bring Israel from bondage had its inception in prayer (Exodus 2:23-25; 3:9.)

September 11, 2001, the Boston Marathon bombing, the San Bernadino massacre and other such attacks worldwide were assaults from hell, planned by demonic spirits, and carried out by their representatives on earth. Today's terrorist attacks in Israel are a result of those same evil powers, ones that cannot be defeated without prayer. Praying saints are God's agents to carry out His will on earth. America is helpless without prayer, as is Israel. If Daniel and Abraham found it necessary to pray regularly, and if Jesus said that He could do nothing without prayer, then we surely cannot hope to accomplish anything of eternal significance and value without prayer.

A Christian who refuses to pray is not unlike a swimmer refusing to get in the water. All the talking in the world of how much we know about swimming will only bring those we are trying to influence to laughter. For a Christian, to refuse to make prayer the number one priority is like saying to the Islamic State, "We refuse to fight; you win!" Our weapons of war and our Commander in Chief are waiting to win the battle; we only need to speak the Word:

> For the word of God *is* living and powerful, and sharper than any two-edged sword, piercing even to the division of soul and spirit, and of joints and marrow, and is a discerner of the thoughts and intents of the heart. (Hebrews 4:12, NKJV)

Darkness flees when we pray! Demons tremble when we pray. Heaven moves when we pray, and angels receive assignments when we pray. Prayer affects three realms: The Divine, the Angelic, and the Human. Without prayer, demons rule uncontested (see Ephesians 6.) Prayer turns the head of God, penetrates the heart of God, and moves His hand.

Hannah's petition for a son (see 1 Samuel 1:11) began a great prayer movement in Israel. Her prayers brought about the birth of Samuel the Prophet who would anoint a shepherd boy to become the king of Israel and rule over the City of David. Samuel was a man of prayer. He stood before the people on one occasion and said, "Far be it from me that I should sin against the Lord in ceasing to pray for you." (1 Samuel 12:23, NKJV)

We cannot make contact with God without prayer. If we don't make contact with Him, no matter how sincere our intentions, we will see no change in the circumstances of our life.

When King Solomon prayed at the dedication of the Temple, God exhibited His great power and revealed His plan (see 2 Chronicles 7:12-15). Solomon called unto God in prayer and Jehovah was there:

> Then you shall call, and the Lord will answer;
> You shall cry, and He will say, "Here I am."
> (Isaiah 58:9, NKJV)

King Solomon prophesied that a mighty national revival

was coming to Israel. It has not happened yet; and it will only come through the power of prayer. You and I can help usher in that revival through prayer.

Hezekiah was another example of God's response to prayer and repentance. During a dark hour of Israel's history, the Assyrians demanded heavy tribute from the king.

> And Hezekiah prayed to the LORD: "LORD, the God of Israel, enthroned between the cherubim, you alone are God over all the kingdoms of the earth. You have made heaven and earth. Give ear, LORD, and hear; open your eyes, LORD, and see; listen to the words Sennacherib has sent to ridicule the living God. "It is true, LORD, that the Assyrian kings have laid waste these nations and their lands. They have thrown their gods into the fire and destroyed them, for they were not gods but only wood and stone, fashioned by human hands. Now, LORD our God, deliver us from his hand, so that all the kingdoms of the earth may know that you alone, LORD, are God." (II Kings 19:14-19, NIV)

In response, Hezekiah stripped the Temple of its gold and silver in order to meet the demand. Still, that was not enough. The Assyrians mounted an attack against the city. Hezekiah bowed before God and prayed, then God responded with an amazing victory! He sent a plague that killed 185,000 Assyrian soldiers.

In great gratitude for God's mercy, Hezekiah cleansed, repaired, and reopened the Temple of God. Worship of Jehovah was restored; daily sacrifices were resumed; the Passover Feast was again celebrated by the nation.

The world has been trying to find an answer to the ongoing crisis in the Bible land. That answer is in your hands and mine—through intercessory prayer:

> You do not have because you do not ask. (James 4:2, NIV)

> So I say to you, ask, and it will be given to you; seek, and you will find; knock, and it will be opened to you. For everyone who asks receives, and he who seeks finds, and to him who knocks it will be opened. (Luke 11:9-10, NIV)

You may be like the prophet Jonah who did everything *but* pray. He knew what God wanted him to do, but kept resisting. Jonah fled, and ended up in the belly of a big fish. There he cried out to God against whom he had sinned. God intervened and caused the fish to vomit Jonah out onto dry land. Even the fish of the sea are subject to the power of prayer! When those in Nineveh saw this stinking, praying prophet, they repented quickly and God sent revival.

Author and minister, John Paul Jackson wrote of the importance of a dedicated intercessory prayer life:

> Prayer is our cry to God for His help. It is the recognition of our weakness and His omnipotence. It is the belief that God, who is all-powerful, hears and acts on our behalf. When we refuse to pray, nothing happens. Change only occurs when we pray for His Kingdom to come and His will to be done. God allows many of His resolutions to be placed on hold because we will not prayer.[53]

It is time for the Body of Christ to pray without ceasing for the nation of Israel, and to put on the whole armor of God to stand firm against the Enemy. Satan, you can't have Israel!

PRAYER FOR ISRAEL:
(FROM NEHEMIAH 1:5-11A)

I pray, LORD God of heaven, O great and awesome God, *You* who keep *Your* covenant and mercy with those who love You and observe Your commandments, please let Your ear be attentive and Your eyes open, that You may hear the prayer of Your servant which I pray before You now, day and night, for the children of Israel Your servants, and confess the sins of the children of Israel which we have sinned against You. Both my father's house and I have sinned. We have acted very corruptly against You, and have not kept the commandments, the statutes, nor the ordinances which You commanded of Your servant Moses. Remember, I pray, the word that You commanded Your servant Moses, saying, '*If* you are unfaithful, I will scatter you among the nations; but *if* you return to Me, and keep My commandments and do them, though some of you were cast out to the farthest part of the heavens, *yet* I will gather them from there, and bring them to the place which I have chosen as a dwelling for My name.' Now these *are* Your servants and Your people, whom You have redeemed by Your great power, and by Your strong hand. O Lord, I pray, please let Your ear be attentive to the prayer of Your servant, and to the prayer of Your servants who desire to fear Your name. . .

SCRIPTURES FOR STUDY:

Psalm 34:17	Psalm 107:6	Psalm 40:17
Psalm 50:15	Psalm 34:4	Galatians 5:1
John 8:32	Romans 6:7-19	II Peter 2:9

STAND WITH ISRAEL

*Their descendants will be recognized and honored
among the nations. Everyone will realize that
they are a people the Lord has blessed.*

ISAIAH 61:9, NLT

IF THE REVEALED WILL of God and the record of
history mean anything to followers of the Jewish Messiah—
as they must—we can only conclude that Christians have a
God-ordained duty to love and support the Jewish people
in every possible way. More than a duty, it should be
considered a great privilege to bless the people of the
Book who have blessed us; especially by being the chan-
nels through which our sacred Bible and our precious
salvation have come to us.

Jesus Himself said that the Son of Man will pass judgment on the nations when He comes to rule on His glorious
throne as King of Kings:

> When the Son of Man comes in his glory, and
> all the angels with him, then he will sit on his
> glorious throne. (Matthew 25:31, ESV)

He went on to reveal that the main criteria for judgment would be how Gentiles treated His brethren in the House of Israel:

> And the King will answer them, "Truly, I say to
> you, as you did it to one of the least of these my
> brothers, you did it to me." (Matthew 25:40, ESV)

Of course, we who are faithful followers of the Great Shepherd are the Lord's spiritual brethren. Jesus' Jewish kin, however, will always be His basic family stock, and thus His particular brethren. There is good reason to believe that these are the ones to whom the Lord referred in Matthew 25.

Paul confirms that Christians are to especially bless the Jewish people. Indeed, these Scriptures reveal that Jewish Believers in Jesus—who are once again greatly multiplying in our day—should be the direct recipients of financial blessings from Gentile Believers:

> For it pleased those from Macedonia and Achaia

> to make a certain contribution for the poor among the saints who are in Jerusalem. It pleased them indeed, and they are their debtors. For if the Gentiles have been partakers of their spiritual things, their duty is also to minister to them in material things. (Romans 15:26-27, NIV)

Christians have been blessed beyond words by being grafted into the rich olive tree of Israel. Therefore, we must minister to the Jewish people in the Promised Land in many ways, but especially by actively upholding their right to live there. This is doubly important since widespread anti-Semitism has again reared its ugly head in recent years.

We Christians have a date with destiny! The Church cannot fulfill its eternal purpose if it is not salt and light to Israel (see Acts 1:8). When we support Israel, we are standing with the only nation created by an act of God: The royal land grant that was given to Abraham and his seed through Isaac and Jacob, with an everlasting and unconditional covenant.

> My mercy will I keep for him for evermore,
> and my covenant shall stand fast with him.

His seed also will I make to endure forever, and his throne as the days of heaven. If his children forsake my law, and walk not in my judgments; If they break my statutes, and keep not my commandments; then will I visit their transgression with the rod, and their iniquity with stripes. Nevertheless my loving kindness will I not utterly take from him, nor suffer my faithfulness to fail. My covenant will I not break, nor alter the thing that is gone out of my lips. Once have I sworn by my holiness that I will not lie unto David. His seed shall endure forever, and his throne as the sun before me. It shall be established forever as the moon, and as a faithful witness in heaven. Selah. (Psalm 89:28-37)

In December 1988, I flew to Geneva, Switzerland, and checked into the Hilton Hotel. I believed God would open doors with leaders of nations, and to my amazement, I was allowed into the facility where the General Assembly meetings were being held.

When I arrived in my room, the phone was ringing. It was my friend Reuven Hecht from the prime minister's office. I was asked to speak in defense of Israel on the following day. At the podium, I lifted my Bible heavenward and declared, "This is the final Word; it is non-negotiable. The land belongs to God Almighty, and He has decided its destiny."

At Camp David in July 2002, President Clinton almost succeeded in dividing Jerusalem. He placed a pen in the hand of PLO Chairman Yasser Arafat urging him to sign the agreement that would have accomplished that. Arafat refused to sign. The president was shocked. If Arafat had complied, Jerusalem would have been divided. All Christian sites would now be under Islamic rule of law! This includes Mount Calvary and the Garden Tomb, and even the Christians who live there. The Bible says Jerusalem will be in the hands of the Jewish people when Messiah returns. America was challenging God Almighty and His prophetic plan. Not a wise thing to do.

Why did Arafat not sign the agreement? He wanted not only ALL of the Temple Site, but ALL of Israel's land! The sons of Ishmael live in the desert, and run their oppressive governments by the bullet, not the ballot. Those who take a stand against Israel fight God Almighty. The son of Abraham and Hagar will not win in a battle against God Almighty. Why? For thousands of years, the offspring of

Ishmael have spoken curses over Jacob's seed. When the wars of the Middle East have finally ended, Jacob's sons will rule. Who will win the conflict in the Middle East? Those who bless Israel will be triumphant. Who will lose the battle in the Middle East? Those who fight the State of Israel will go down in defeat. God created Israel; God defends Israel.

Consider the nation of Egypt. Joseph birthed a generation of wealth. After his death, there arose a Pharaoh who persecuted the Jewish people, and enslaved them. He not only starved them, but also drowned their children in the river Nile. Why? He was trying to control that nation. As a result of Pharaoh's enslavement of His people, God sent plagues. The first-born child in every Egyptian home was slain by the Death Angel. In some Egyptian homes, that meant every male family member died.

For every Hebrew baby that died in the Nile, an Egyptian child died. For every Hebrew father who died at the oppressive hands of the Egyptian overseers, an Egyptian father died. For every Hebrew mother who died of starvation, or of a broken heart, an Egyptian mother grieved the loss of family. What you do to another, God will cause to come to you.

An angry, bitter Pharaoh gathered his terrified, demoralized troops, and pursued the Hebrew children as they departed Egypt. He led his army directly into the path of God's wrath, and all drowned in the Red Sea. Overnight, Egypt became a land of poverty and disease. It remains that way 4,000 years later... because it chose to curse the Jewish people, rather than bless them.

In the twenty-first century Israel faces a much more dire threat than from Hamas, Hezbollah, the PLO, or the Islamic State; it faces the possibility of annihilation by Iran, a country that plans to soon be armed with nuclear weapons.

Most nations of the world agree that a freeze on Iran's nuclear program is absolutely necessary for a peaceful Middle East. The halt of production of both highly-enriched uranium and a means to deliver an atomic bomb is essential. Yet, Iran has continued to ignore the warnings of world leaders as well as those of the International Atomic Energy Agency and the United Nations. As a result, strict sanctions have been instituted as a means to end Iranian nuclear pursuits. But those sanctions are slowly being eased, and it has become unlikely that even they can be properly and fully policed.

The country most vocal about the danger Iran presents to the world is the smallest of nations in the crosshairs—Israel. It is a predicament no twenty-first century nation should have to face—annihilation. Only one member-nation in the United Nations has another member calling for it to be "wiped off the map"—Israel. There is little reason to believe it is merely an idle threat as it is so often repeated by Iran's leaders.

An article posted on Alef website, one with ties to the Iranian supreme leader, calls for the destruction of Jews everywhere:

> ... the opportunity must not be lost to remove "this corrupting material. It is a "'jurispru-dential justification" to kill all the Jews and annihilate Israel, and in that, the Islamic government of Iran must take the helm... Khamenei announced that Iran will support any nation or group that attacks the "cancerous tumor" of Israel. Though his statement was seen by some in the West as fluff, there is substance behind it... The article then quotes the Quran (Albaghara 2:191-193): "And slay them wherever ye find them, and drive them out of the places

whence they drove you out, for persecution [of Muslims] is worse than slaughter [of non-believers]... and fight them until persecution is no more, and religion is for Allah."[54]

Repeated calls for the destruction of Israel issued from Tehran were at their loudest and most vociferous under the leadership of former President Mahmoud Ahmadinejad. With the advent of a new president in August 2013, the rhetoric was dialed back a bit, but few believe Iran's intentions towards the Jewish state have been rescinded. With all the calls for détente with Iran, only one scripture comes to mind:

When people are saying, "Everything is peaceful and secure," then disaster will fall on them as suddenly as a pregnant woman's labor pains begin. And there will be no escape. (I Thessalonians 5:3, NLT)

There is little doubt that the desire to destroy Israel is foremost in the minds of Iran's Supreme Leader Ali Khamenei and his henchmen as has been proven by the continual supply of arms from Iran to her proxies in Syria, Hezbollah in Lebanon and Hamas in Gaza. Rocket attacks launched from both Lebanon and Gaza have plagued Israeli towns in the past; it is unthinkable that Israel may soon be faced with the ramifications of a nuclear-armed Iran.

The United States has been very vocal about what is and is not acceptable from Iran but it has been all talk and little, if any, substance. The saber-rattling has been mere noise. The conclusion might very well be that the U.S. is totally intimidated by Iranian oratory. Why would anyone make that assumption? Iran's nuclear program has grown from one centrifuge to as many as 3,000 working to more quickly enrich uranium. This has been accomplished while most world leaders have stood by wringing their collective hands. It appears that Israel alone has been left to make a stand against the threats issued by the supreme ayatollah in charge in Tehran.

Even scarier is the thought of how the landscape in the Middle East would be changed if dominated by a nuclear-armed Iran. That notwithstanding, it is one thing to aver that a nuclear-armed Iran is unacceptable and enact sanctions, but quite another to take the steps necessary to stop the achievement of that goal. Thus far, all the grandiloquence has done nothing but cause sniggers behind closed doors in Tehran.

Perhaps the question of greatest import is this: Would the U.S. stand with Israel if it were overtly targeted by Iran? Maybe; maybe not. The difference may be measured by how direct the threat would be to the United States, the country the Ayatollah Khomeini labeled the "Great Satan." The time to close the barn door is not after the horses have galloped down the road. The time to stop Iran's nuclear threats is before the first atomic weapon rolls off the assembly line. No one seems to know exactly when that will be, or if perhaps it has already occurred.

Of greater concern to Israel is the lessening of sanctions against Iran. Successful talks in Geneva in November 2013 were aimed at doing just that if concrete changes were made to Iran's nuclear program. Unfortunately, with so much being done clandestinely how can anyone be certain of compliance by Iran's rulers?

According to the security and intelligence news service, The Debka file, Iran has already stretched the limits of—if not broken the nuclear agreement:

> In defiance of the international arms embargo, Iran last week placed an order with Moscow for a huge fleet of 100 Russian IL78 MKI tanker

aircraft (NATO: Midas) for refueling its air force in mid-flight, thereby extending its range to 7,300 km. This is reported exclusively by debkafile from its military and intelligence sources. The transaction runs contrary to the terms of the nuclear accord the six world powers and Iran signed in Vienna earlier this month. These tanker planes can simultaneously refuel six to eight warplanes. Their acquisition brings Israel, 1.200km away—as well the rest of the Middle East—within easy range of Iranian aerial bombardment. It also puts Iran's air force ahead of Israel's in terms of the quantity and range of its refueling capacity.[55]

Prime Minister Benjamin Netanyahu said of the deal:

What was reached...in Geneva is not a historic agreement, it is a historic mistake....the world became a much more dangerous place because the most dangerous regime in the world made a significant step in obtaining the most dangerous weapons in the world....I want to clarify that Israel will not let Iran develop nuclear military capability.[56]

Leaders of Muslim countries with largely Sunni populations—Saudi Arabia, Kuwait, the United Arab Emirates,
Bahrain, Qatar, Egypt and Jordan—were coldly silent
on the accord reached in Geneva. Chairman Abdullah
al-Askar of Saudi Arabia's Shoura Council, a group that
advises the Saudi government on policy said:

> I am afraid Iran will give up something to get
> something else from the big powers in terms
> of regional politics — and I'm worrying about
> giving Iran more space or a freer hand in the
> region. The government of Iran, month after
> month, has proven that it has an ugly agenda
> in the region, and in this regard no one in the
> region will sleep and assume things are going
> smoothly.[57]

Why would Iran's leaders, who have no shortage of
insolence and audacity, agree to suspend nuclear enrich-
ment for any period of time? Simple: the money to keep
their program running has been severely compromised
by the sanctions. There is speculation that the $7 billion
in sanction relief will not benefit the Iranian people, but
will go directly into the coffers of Supreme Leader Ali

Khamenei's Revolutionary Guard Corps. Such a lofty sum would purchase a lot of equipment for the various centrifuges in the land of the ayatollahs.

One thing is certain: If the U.S. hopes to be blessed by God Almighty, her loyalty must be to Israel and not to her enemies; her willingness to act in support of Israel, unwavering. Sadly, the occupant of the White House, regardless of party affiliation, seems not to understand that biblical precept.

Israel is under siege! Demons are not required to clear customs, but no weapon in the arsenal is more formidable than the will and courage of the God-fearing, praying Believer. Will you take up the challenge today and shout, "SATAN, YOU CAN'T HAVE ISRAEL!"

BLESSINGS FOR ISRAEL:

I SAMUEL 12:22, NIV

For the sake of his great name the LORD will not reject his people, because the LORD was pleased to make you his own.

PSALM 17:6-9, NIV

I call on you, my God, for you will answer me; turn your ear to me and hear my prayer. Show me the wonders of your great love, you who save by your right hand those who take refuge in you from their foes. Keep me as the apple of your eye; hide me in the shadow of your wings from the wicked who are out to destroy me, from my mortal enemies who surround me.

PSALM 17:16-19, NIV

As for me, I call to God, and the LORD saves me. Evening, morning and noon I cry out in distress, and he hears my voice. He rescues me unharmed from the battle waged against me, even though many oppose me. God, who is enthroned from of old, who does not change—he will hear them and humble them, because they have no fear of God.

PSALM 25:22, NIV

Deliver Israel, O God, from all their troubles!

PSALM 100, NIV

Shout for joy to the LORD, all the earth. Worship the LORD with gladness; come before him with joyful songs. Know that the LORD is God. It is he who made us, and we are his; we are his people, the sheep of his pasture. Enter his gates with thanksgiving and his courts with praise; give thanks to him and praise his name. For the LORD is good and his love endures forever; his faithfulness continues through all generations.

PSALM 102:12-16, NIV

But you, LORD, sit enthroned forever; your renown endures through all generations. You will arise and have compassion on Zion, for it is time to show favor to her; the appointed time has come. For her stones are dear to your servants; her very dust moves them to pity. The nations will fear the name of the LORD, all the kings of the earth will revere your glory. For the LORD will rebuild Zion and appear in his glory.

PSALM 122:6-8, NIV

Pray for the peace of Jerusalem: "May those who love you be secure. May there be peace within your walls and security within your citadels." For the sake of my family and friends, I will say, "Peace be within you."

PROVERBS 16:7, NIV

When the LORD takes pleasure in anyone's way, he causes their enemies to make peace with them.

ISAIAH 45:3-4, NIV

I will give you hidden treasures, riches stored in secret places, so that you may know that I am the LORD, the God of Israel, who summons you by name. For the sake of Jacob my servant, of Israel my chosen, summon you by name and bestow on you a title of honor. . .

ISAIAH 45:17-18, NIV

But Israel will be saved by the LORD with an everlasting salvation; you will never be put to shame or disgraced, to ages everlasting. For this is what the LORD says—he who created the heavens, he is God; he who fashioned and made the earth, he founded it; he did not create it to be empty, but formed it to be inhabited—he says: "I am the LORD, and there is no other.

JOEL 3:16, NIV

The LORD will roar from Zion and thunder from Jerusalem; the earth and the heavens will tremble. But the LORD will be a refuge for his people, a stronghold for the people of Israel.

ENDNOTES

1.   http://dictionary.reference.com/browse/asymmetrical--warfare; accessed December 2015.

2.   "Church must repent of the sin of anti-Semitism," Assist News Service, July 16, 2013, http://www.christiantoday.com/article/church.must.repent.of.sin.of.anti.semitism/33198.htm; accessed December 2015.

3.   Charles Krauthammer, *The Weekly Standard*, May 11, 1998, http://www.eternaltreeofpeace.com/; accessed October 2013.

4.   Eric R. Mandel, "Is the United Nations Anti-Semitic?" The Jerusalem Post, July 7, 2014, http://www.jpost.com/Opinion/Op-Ed-Contributors/Is-the-United-Nations-anti-Semitic-361842; accessed November 2015.

5.   Elli Wohlgelernteri, "One Day that Shook the World," *The Jerusalem Post*, 30 April 1998; accessed October 2013.

6.   George Gilder, *The Israel Test* (Minneapolis, MN: Richard Vigilante Books, 2009), pp. 234-235.

7.   David Naggar, "The Case for a Larger Israel," http://alargerisrael.blogspot.com/; accessed October 2013.

8.   Derek Prince, http://www.prayerforallpeople.com/jerusalem.html; accessed November 2015.

9.   Israel Matzav, "I will bless those who bless you, and I will curse him that curses you," Thursday, April 22, 2010, http://israelmatzav.blogspot.com/search?q=I+will+bless+them+that+bless+you; accessed June 2013.

10. Martin Gilbert, *Churchill and the Jews* (Toronto: McClelland & Steward, 2007), pp. 160-161.

11. Alfred Lord Tennyson, http://thinkexist.com/quotation/more_ things_are_wrought_by_prayer_than_this_world/12679.html; accessed October 2013.

12. George Bakalav, "10 Reasons Why Christians Should Support Israel—whether it's Popular or Not," January 20, 2009, http:// voices.yahoo.com/10-reasons-why-christians-support-israel- whether-2498811.html; accessed November 2013.

13. Senator James Inhofe (R-OK), "Seven Reasons Why Israel has the Right to Her Land," http://www.senate.gov/~inhofe/fl030402. html; accessed September 2013.

14. Fuel for Truth; http://www.fuelfortruth.org/thetruth/truth_10. asp; accessed April 2010.

15. Christopher Wise, *Derrida, Africa and the Middle East* (New York, NY: St. Martin's Press, 2009), p. 59.

16. Phillip Misselwitz and Tim Rieniets, *City of Collision: Jerusalem and the Principles of Conflict Urbanism;* (Germany: Die Deutsche Bibliothek, 2006), p. 49.

17. "The Mists of Antiquity 2000-1000 BC, Teddy Kollek and Moshe Pearlman, *Jerusalem: Sacred City of Mankind*, Steimatzky Ltd., Jerusalem, 1991, http://cojs.org/cojswiki/The_Mists_of_ Antiquity_2000-1000_BC%2C_Teddy_Kollek_and_Moshe_ Pearlman%2C_Jerusalem:_Sacred_City_of_Mankind%2C_ Steimatzky_Ltd.%2C_Jerusalem%2C_1991; accessed November 2013.

18. Amikam Elad, "Why did 'Abd al-Malik Build the Dome of the Rock?" Bayt-al-Maqdis: 'Abd al-Malik's Jerusalem, ed. Julian Raby and Jeremy Johns (Oxford: Oxford University Press, 1992), vol. 1, p. 48.

19. Dr. John MacArthur, "Is God Finished with Israel, Part 1," "http://www.gty.org/Resources/Sermons/1319, accessed December 2015.

20. Dr. Billy Graham, "Jesus Willingly Gave His Life for Us," Chicago Tribune, April 5, 2012, http://articles.chicagotribune.com/2012-04-05/features/sns-201203130000--tms--bgrahamctnym-a20120405apr05_1_sins-eternal-life-god; accessed October 2013.

21. "Judaism Now," http://judaism-now.blogspot.com/2009/09/is-god-man.html; accessed October 2013.

22. Peter Wehner, "Israel and Evangelical Christians, Commentary Magazine, October 28, 2013, http://www.commentarymagazine.com/2013/10/28/israel-and-evangelical-christians/#more-835429; accessed October 2013.

23. Martin Niemöller: "First they came for the Socialists..." http://www.ushmm.org/wlc/en/article.php?ModuleId=10007392; accessed October 2015.

24. Cohn, Norman (1966), Warrant for Genocide: The Myth of the Jewish World-Conspiracy and the Protocols of the Elder of Zion (New York: Harper & Row, 2006), pp. 32–36.

25. "Hamas Covenant," Yale, 1988: "Today it is Palestine, tomorrow it will be one country or another. The Zionist plan is limitless. After Palestine, the Zionists aspire to expand from the Nile to the Euphrates. When they will have digested the region they overtook, they will aspire to further expansion, and so on. Their plan is embodied in the 'Protocols of the Elders of Zion', and their present conduct is the best proof of what we are saying."; accessed May 2013.

26. Islamic Antisemitism in Historical Perspective (PDF), Anti-Defamation League, 276 kB; accessed October 2013

27. Omri Ceren, "O Beloved Belgium, Sacred Land of Anti-Semitism," *Commentary Magazine*, May 17, 2011, http://www.commentarymagazine.com/2011/05/17/belgian-minister-says-to-forget-about-nazis/; accessed October 2013.

28. Oren Dorell, "Tiny Belgium is a terrorist crossroad," *USA Today*, January 17, 2015, http://www.usatoday.com/story/news/world/2015/01/16/belgium-terrorist-crossroad/21866187/; accessed December 2015.

29. John Goldingay, *Isaiah* (Grand Rapids, MI, Baker Books, 2001), 223.

30. Walter Brueggemann, *Isaiah 40-66* (Louisville, KY: Westminster John Knox Press, 1998), p18.

31. Barry Rubin, "The Region: All Israel, all the Time," *The Jerusalem Post*, August 23, 2010, http://www.jpost.com/Opinion/Op-Ed-Contributors/The-Region-All-Israel-all-the-time; accessed October 2013.

32. Bernard Avishai, *The Hebrew Republic: How Secular Democracy and Global Enterprise will Bring Israel Peace at Last* (New York: Harcourt, 2008), pp. 198-201.

33. Paul C. Merkley, "Christian Attitudes: A Bird's Eye View," *Arutz Sheva*, March 14, 2004; http://www.israelnationalnews.com/Articles/Article.aspx/3444; accessed August 2011. (NOTE: WCC Press Releases issued July 1997, October 4, 1997, November 1997; March 1998; September 21, 2001.)

34. Global Ministries of the United Methodist Church; http://gbgm-umc.org/global_news/full_article.cfm?articleid=694; accessed January 2012.

35. Ibid.

36. http://www.prayingscriptures.com/jerusalem.shtml; accessed November 2016.

37. Quoted by George Gilder in *The Israel Test* (Minneapolis, MN: Richard Vigilante Books, 2009), p. 22.

38. Arthur W. Pink, "The Death of the Firstborn," Old Testament Study: Exodus 11:1-10, http://www.scripturestudies.com/Vol11/K10/ot.html; accessed November 2013.

39. Irwin N. Graulich, "Why America Supports Israel," FrontPageMag.com, December 20, 2002; http://archive.frontpagemag.com/readArticle.aspx?ARTID=20579; accessed January 2012.

40. Paul Goldman, "Dying 4-year old girl finds life-savers in the land of the enemy," http://worldnews.nbcnews.com/_news/2013/05/26/18445610-dying-4-year-old-girl-finds-life-savers-in-land-of-the-enemy?lite, May 2013; accessed June 2013.

41. David Miller, "Intelligent 'Wrapping Paper' Heals Broken Bones in Half the Time," December 31, 2013; http://news.yahoo.com/blogs/this-could-be-big-abc-news/intelligent-wrapping-paper-heals-broken-bones-half-time-190710297.html?vp=1; accessed January 1, 2014.

42. Marcella Rosen, "65 years of innovations from Israel," May 9, 2013, *The Jewish Observer*, http://jewishobservernashville.org/2013/05/09/65-years-of-innovations-from-israel/; accessed June 2013.

43. See the full list of innovations and inventions at http://jewishobservernashville.org/2013/05/09/65-years-of-innovations-from-israel/.

44. "Nobel Prize in Literature 2002," Nobel Foundation; accessed June 2013.

45. "The Nobel Peace Prize for 1986: Elie Wiesel," Nobelprize.org, 14 October 1986; accessed June 2013.

46. Victoria J. Barnett, "The Role of the Churches: Compliance and Confrontation," http://archive.adl.org/braun/dim_14_1_role_church.html#.Vl8M4f2FM3E; accessed December 2015.

47. "Professor Robert Aumann: He's Got Game," *The Jerusalem Post*, November 1, 2005, www.jpost.com/servlet/Satellite?cid=1129540643006&pagename= JPost%2FJPArticle%2FShowFull; accessed June 2013.

48. Robert Aumann, http://en.wikipedia.org/wiki/Robert_Aumann, accessed June 2013.

49. http://www.quotationcollection.com/author/Ernest-Hemingway/quotes; accessed June 2013.

50. "BDS Victories," http://www.bdsmovement.net/victories#sthash.2s6AEwL0.dpuf; accessed August 2015.

51. Rachel Zoll, "United Church of Christ to divest over Israeli policies in occupied Palestinian territories," Star Tribune, June 30, 2015, http://www.startribune.com/ucc-church-to-divest-over-israeli-treatment-of-palestinians/310966861/; accessed December 2015.

52. "Church must repent of the sin of anti-Semitism," Assist News Service, July 16, 2013, http://www.christiantoday.com/article/church.must.repent.of.sin.of.anti.semitism/33198.htm; accessed December 2015.

53. John Paul Jackson, "Prayer and Spiritual Warfare," http://www.streamsministries.com/resources/supernatural/prayer-spiritual-warfare; accessed December 2015.

54. Reza Kahlili, "Ayatollah: Kill all Jews, Annihilate Israel," World Net Daily, February 5, 2012, http://www.wnd.com/2012/02/ayatollah-kill-all-jews-annihilate-israel/#dUomRSFSddGwcqWP.99; accessed November 2013.

55. "Iran already violating the agreement," http://freerepublic.com/focus/f-news/3315366/posts; accessed December 2015.

56. Josep Federman, "Netanyahu: Iran Nuclear Deal a 'historic mistake'," *Huffington Post*, November 25, 2013, http://www. huffingtonpost.com/2013/11/24/netanyahu-iran-deal-israel-nuclear_n_4332906.html; accessed November 2013.

57. "Arabs not allied with Iran not quiet over nuclear deal," *USAToday*, November 24, 2013, http://www.usatoday.com/story/news/world/2013/11/24/iran-nuclear-deal-arab-reactions/3691289/; accessed November 2013.

ABRAHAM'S LAND GRANT

THE UNITED KINGDOM OF ISRAEL
(AROUND THE TIME OF SAUL & DAVID)

MODERN-DAY ISRAEL

MICHAEL DAVID EVANS

is a #1 *New York Times* bestselling author
of more than 60 books. His articles have appeared
in newspapers worldwide, including *USA Today*,
The Jerusalem Post, *Washington Times*, and
the *Wall Street Journal*. He has appeared on
hundreds of USA television and radio shows.

Evans was the first American to predict the
occurrence of a 9-11 more than a decade before it
happened and also the first to predict the rise of ISIS,
radical Islam's new caliphate in his 2007 #1 *New York
Times*' bestseller *The Final Move Beyond Iraq*.

Evans is the founder of the Jerusalem Prayer Team,
the Ten Boom Holocaust Center in Haarlem, Holland
and the Friends of Zion Museum in Jerusalem.

BOOKS BY: MIKE EVANS

Israel: America's Key to Survival
Save Jerusalem
The Return
Jerusalem D.C.
Purity and Peace of Mind
Who Cries for the Hurting?
Living Fear Free
I Shall Not Want
Let My People Go
Jerusalem Betrayed
Seven Years of Shaking: A Vision
The Nuclear Bomb of Islam
Jerusalem Prophecies
Pray For Peace of Jerusalem
America's War: The Beginning
of the End
The Jerusalem Scroll
The Prayer of David
The Unanswered Prayers of Jesus
God Wrestling
The American Prophecies
Beyond Iraq: The Next Move
The Final Move beyond Iraq
Showdown with Nuclear Iran
Jimmy Carter: The Liberal Left
and World Chaos
Atomic Iran
Cursed
Betrayed
The Light
Corrie's Reflections & Meditations
The Revolution
The Final Generation
Seven Days
The Locket

GAMECHANGER SERIES:
GameChanger
Samson Option
The Four Horsemen

THE PROTOCOLS SERIES:
The Protocols
The Candidate

Persia: The Final Jihad
Jerusalem
The History of Christian Zionism
Countdown
Ten Boom: Betsie, Promise of God
Commanded Blessing
Born Again: 1948
Born Again: 1967
Presidents in Prophecy
Stand with Israel
Prayer, Power and Purpose
Turning Your Pain Into Gain
Christopher Columbus, Secret Jew
Living in the F.O.G.
Finding Favor with God
Finding Favor with Man
Unleashing God's Favor
The Jewish State: The Volunteers
See You in New York
Friends of Zion: Patterson &
Wingate
The Columbus Code
The Temple
Satan, You Can't Have My Country!
Satan, You Can't Have Israel!

COMING SOON:
Netanyahu
Lights in the Darkness

TO PURCHASE, CONTACT: orders@timeworthybooks.com
P. O. BOX 30000, PHOENIX, AZ 85046